M000074484

Twisting Minds

Tessonja Odette

Published by Crystal Moon Press, 2020.

TWISTING MINDS

First edition. January 31, 2020.

Written by Tessonja Odette.

CHAPTER ONE

"Claire, are you ready to talk about Darren?" Dr. Shelia asks in her quiet voice.

I'm not ready but can't bring myself to say so. Instead, I swallow the lump in my throat and stare at the bright white ceiling of Dr. Shelia's office. The silence grows heavy between us as my mind spins with anxiety.

How did I get here?

How did I become this?

"Relax, Claire."

My muscles are tensed, fingers clenched into fists at my sides, nails digging painfully into my palms. I close my eyes and release a deep breath, shifting my shoulders as I try to relax into the hard couch beneath me. Just as my heart begins to slow its racing, a light whirring sound buzzes past my ear. Irritation courses through me as I fight the urge to swat at it. The microscopic cameras have been a constant in my life for over six months now, circling me like an invisible halo. Still, I've never gotten used to the sound of one getting so close.

Who is on the other side of that camera? Is anyone watching? What do they see? A girl falling apart? Or one being put back together?

"Take your time," Dr. Shelia says, drawing my attention back to her. "Think about him from the beginning. Can you do that?"

I can't think about him. Not yet. Not when it means letting him go. Because letting go of Darren means letting go of the only man I've ever loved. It means letting go of the memories

I've been clinging to like a life raft for months. It means accepting that I've gone crazy.

Completely, utterly, certifiably crazy.

What would my mom say if she could see me now?

How did I get here?

How did I become this empty shell of a being?

Dr. Shelia would say I'm healthy now, for the things I'm about to confess to her. But I don't feel healthy. I feel like I'm losing something. No—that I've already lost something. And I have. So many things. My privacy. My rights as a citizen. My mom. My sanity. My happiness.

Not too long ago, I *was* happy. Briefly.

Then again, can it really be called happiness if the thing that made me feel that way was never real?

I'm not ready to answer that. I'm not ready to let go.

CHAPTER TWO
Six months ago

My mom isn't coming back. She's gone forever. I'm completely on my own.

The realization strikes me so hard it forces me to squeeze the arms of my chair to keep me from careening to the floor. I don't feel like I'm going to cry. Instead, I feel like I'm being sucked into a black chasm of emptiness. I'd prefer to cry. Or grieve. Even fear would be preferable to this.

"Claire Harper," calls a woman behind a long desk at the far end of the waiting room. I see my name flashing above station eight and approach the glass window. Without acknowledging me, the woman stares at the screen in front of her. "Your probation officer will see you now. Room 402, eighth floor."

I nod my thanks and head to the elevators at the far end of the lobby. Once inside the lift, I turn to face the glass panel behind me, looking over an expanse of flat ground crisscrossed with rail tracks leading to the Select District. The Select city towers reach high in the distance, jewel-like windows catching the pink and gold light of the setting sun.

I purposefully avoid looking to the far north end of the city, where the Select housing centers are located. Even at this distance, I could probably pick out the apartment tower where I lived most of my youth. I never appreciated what I had back then. All I wanted was what my parents wanted. To become Elites. To live in the Elite city in a bigger apartment and go to an Elite school.

If only I knew then how far that wish would make us fall.

The elevator stops, and I sigh before turning my back on the view to face the dim light of the eighth-floor hallway. The Seattle Public Citizen Probation building is probably the nicest building in the Public District, which isn't saying much. But since the probation officers working here are Select citizens, the decor and amenities favor their elevated status. Although, they can't be too elevated in status to be assigned such an undesirable job, working in the Public District. Then again, perhaps the Select citizens enjoy doling out sentences to Public citizens. Citizens like me.

After a few turns, I find the door I'm looking for. 402. I knock, then enter, finding a modestly furnished office with a single desk, a bookcase, and three chairs. In one of those chairs—the one behind the desk—sits a middle-aged man with a ring of strawberry-blond hair surrounding a bald scalp. His eyes meet mine as I enter the room, and he offers me what looks like a forced smile.

"Claire Harper," he says, "I'm Marcus Smith, your assigned probation officer. Have a seat."

I take the only empty seat, next to a smiling woman with a black, angled bob streaked with purple. She's wearing a sweater in an abstract pattern with colors to match her hair and a black mini skirt. Her thigh-high boots sport a six-inch platform and a gold buckle shaped like two linking S's. Stella Song designer boots. That alone tells me she's at least a first rung Elite.

"Claire!" the woman says with far more warmth and enthusiasm than Mr. Smith, extending a hand for me to shake. "I'm Kori Wan."

I grasp her hand, trying to keep a neutral expression on my face when I'd rather scrutinize her with the suspicion I feel. Since when is anyone—Select or Elite—so excited about meeting a Public?

"I have the results of your probationary sentence," Mr. Smith says, drawing my attention back to him.

The blood leaves my face. "And?" I think it might be the first word I've said aloud all day; it comes out like a croak.

He leans back in his chair, elbows perched on its arms as he steeples his fingertips. "Before we get started, I am to remind you of the consequences that come with filing Forgiveness. You were read your rights when you filed, correct? And you accepted the terms?"

I nod, although when I filed, I didn't think I had any choice but to accept them. Filing Forgiveness was mandatory for me, after all. That's what happens when your debt exceeds your lifetime's ability to pay it off.

Mr. Smith continues. "Then I will just remind you that by filing Forgiveness you are now a probationary citizen and have waived your rights as a Public citizen of the United Cities of America. You will be given the accommodations of a Public citizen and will remain on probation until you have served your term. Your term will be complete when you have earned enough credits to pay your reduced fine. Until then you will serve an active sentence, which we will establish today. Agreed?"

"Yes, but..." My words feel like they're stuck in my throat. Do I even want to know the answer to the question I'm about to ask? "What does it mean to waive my rights?"

"You should have asked this before you signed."

"I had to sign." My voice is barely above a whisper.

Mr. Smith sighs. "It means what it sounds like. You don't have rights of citizenship should you step out of line. Follow your terms of probation and you won't have any problems."

I flinch, thinking of the enforcers with their black masks and heavy clubs. Of shouting in the streets. Of men being beaten for saying the wrong thing at the wrong time.

"Marcus!" Kori Wan says with a playful gasp. "You make it sound so scary." She turns to me, smiling. "Claire, it's mostly a technicality. It means that the terms of your probation may be changed at any time, including your active sentence. This would likely only come into play during national emergencies or times of war. You don't need to worry about it, hon."

I look from her to Mr. Smith, who is frowning.

"What?" Kori says with an innocent shrug. "She's my client. I won't have her leaving this meeting scared out of her wits."

"Right," Mr. Smith says. "Let's get back on track." He scans his screen for a few seconds, then faces me. "All I can say is you're lucky you are still underage. That's quite a hefty debt you've inherited from your mother. At your status, it would have taken two lifetimes to pay it off. It's no wonder filing Forgiveness was mandatory for you. If your mother died after you turned eighteen, you would have had a far more severe sentence."

I feel like he wants me to thank him for telling me how lucky I am, but I feel anything but grateful that my mom is dead.

Mr. Smith continues. "Even with you filing for emancipation, you are still being sentenced as a minor, and your job prospects are far better than if you'd been an adult."

A flicker of hope stirs inside me, and I sit forward in my seat. "My emancipation was approved? I'll be able to work?"

"Yes, and you've been approved for your top three requested jobs."

A sigh of relief escapes me, and I close my eyes for a moment. "I was approved for all three jobs?"

"Yes, although before we make it official, I want you to be sure this is something you can commit to. You've never worked before, and you've only been a Public citizen for two years. Your file says you've been an upper rung Select most of your life, and even lived as an Elite for a year when you were eleven."

I nod.

He eyes me with a condescending stare. "Working three jobs might be harder than you expect."

"No, I can do it," I say in a panicked rush. Taking a deep breath, I force myself to regain my composure, and say more calmly, "I am committed to paying off my sentence as quickly as possible."

Mr. Smith shrugs. "Very well, then. Regarding that, filing Forgiveness as a minor brought your inherited debt down from two million credits to 250 thousand credits. With three jobs, you could likely work that off in a matter of years."

Four-to-six years. I already did the math days ago when I tried to anticipate all the different possible outcomes.

He continues. "As for your active sentence, I'll turn you over to Ms. Wan."

Active sentence. My blood goes cold. After the relief of finding out I'll be allowed to work, I've almost forgotten the most daunting part of this meeting. Even with Mr. Smith's assurance that being a minor will work in my favor, I can't help but imagine the worst. If I've been approved for the three jobs I requested, then my sentence can't be job related, which rules out any life-threatening line of work. But I could still be sentenced to serve the military, sent to the war zones or the outlands, used as a decoy force like untrained soldiers often are. I could be used to test experimental medicines with lethal side effects. I could be forced to donate my organs or tissues with no guarantee of my survival.

I'm trembling as I face the woman next to me.

She clasps her hands to her chest with a wide grin. "You're going to serve as a candidate for Reality viewing. Congratulations!"

I stare at her, dumbfounded.

"You're relieved, aren't you? It's really the best probationary sentence anyone can get. I may be biased, being your agent and all—"

"My agent?"

"Of course! You didn't think you'd become a Reality star on your own, did you?"

Being a Reality star doesn't sound much better than any of the other punishments I was imagining, but I don't tell her this. Instead, I ask, "What exactly does it mean? Being a candidate for Reality viewing?"

She beams at me, as if I've asked what her favorite flavor of ice cream is. "The way Reality viewing works under the probationary program is that you will be monitored at all times, resulting in a 24/7 lifestream. Your lifestream will launch immediately in all other cities to all viewers with access to viewing devices and to the Elites here in Seattle. No Public or Select citizen will have access to your lifestream here and that includes you."

I wrinkle my brow. I haven't had a viewing device in years, but even when I did, I never watched some random person's lifestream. Reality viewing was pretty much the height of entertainment when I was growing up, but the shows I watched were curated episodes, not lifestreams of some unknown citizen going about their miserable day.

"Why is viewership restricted?" I ask.

Kori lets out a girlish giggle. "If you and the people you interact with know you have a lifestream, it defeats the purpose, don't you think? The draw of a lifestream is that no one knows it's happening. It's even more important if your lifestream goes viral and you get a show."

I swallow hard. "A show?"

"That's my purpose as your agent. If I can sell your lifestream to a producer, you'll become more than a probationary citizen. You'll be a star. Forget having three jobs. Being a Reality star could help you pay off your probation in no time. You could rise!"

Her words send a ripple up my spine. While I have no interest in being a subject for 24/7 surveillance, I can't help but be reminded of my mother's last words to me.

Rise up, my sweet one. You are worth more than this.

"Oh, don't be afraid," Kori says, misreading the look on my face. "Just be you. I'll do all the work to get your program under the eyes of producers." She leans to the side, shoulders touching mine as a conspiratorial grin plays on her lips. "But if you could make things—you know—*juicy*, the chances of your lifestream getting picked up will be much higher."

I grimace. *Not gonna happen.*

She straightens and takes on a more serious expression. "This could be big. For both of us. I have every intention of making second rung by next year."

It all makes sense now. Her enthusiasm. Her friendliness. She's a first rung Elite, new to the entertainment industry. Entertainment is one of the biggest businesses in Elite society, aside from law, finance, and pharmaceuticals. However, it's hard to make it past first rung in any of those businesses, and even the best fall hard. Accidents can happen to anyone.

Like my parents.

I realize Kori is watching me, an unheard question hanging between us. My eyes snap to hers. "I'm sorry, what did you say?"

She raises a brow at me. "I said, do you have any questions?"

I blink at her, trying to remember what we were talking about. A disquieting thought comes to mind. "Um...will I have a camera crew?"

"Of course not, silly," she says with a giggle. "Camera crews are rare these days, especially since Hunter Ellis...well, you know."

I gulp. Hunter Ellis committed suicide live on his Reality show. His camera crew did nothing to stop him, even going so far as to film closeups of the aftermath for nearly an hour. I was ten at the time. Everyone watched Hunter Ellis back then, young and old. Who wouldn't enjoy the antics of a former celebrity who lost his status to gambling and drug addiction? Seven years later, I can still remember every detail of his final episode.

Hunter, staring at a gun. A hopeless expression. Darkness in his eyes. Death.

"His episode is still the highest viewed of all time, both live and replay. Can you believe that?" Kori's voice is full of yearning, not the disgust I feel inside as I recall the sight of blood and brains splattered over a tabletop. "I wish I'd been his agent."

"I bet you do," I can't help but say.

Kori doesn't seem to catch the bite in my tone. "Anyhow, no you won't have a camera crew. Even though Hunter Ellis' crew was acquitted of all charges and the Ellis Law has remained in effect since, it's just better to avoid them altogether, you know? Plus, it's cheaper."

The Ellis Law. I remember that too. It forbids any crew member from physically interfering with a cast member's actions during the filming of a Reality show. Subjects are simply to be watched. Recorded. Like the nature documentaries from the olden days that Mom used to tell me about.

Kori reaches into a dainty purse and removes something flat, circular, and silver. She presses a latch, and it springs open like a compact, revealing six tiny, silver balls, each the size of an insect, surrounding an equally small, flat, silver disk.

She lifts the disk with her fingertips. "Give me your wrist, Claire."

I frown, turning my wrist toward her, eyes fixed on the disk. "What are you—"

Before I can finish, Kori presses the metal to the inside of my wrist, and with a sharp sting, the disk latches into my skin. I slap my palm over it, my heart racing.

"Relax," Kori says without looking at me. She's pressing her thumb over the center of the compact until six green dots light up next to the metal balls. "It's so the cameras recognize you." The balls shoot out of the silver container and into the air. I try to follow them with my eyes, but I only catch a glimpse of one here and there as they begin to circle me.

The hair rises on my arms and my pulse quickens. I feel suddenly naked. Watched.

Kori closes the compact and slips it back in her purse as she rises to her feet. "That's all from me. You likely won't see me again for a very long time, either once your lifestream gets picked up, or to remove the tracker when your probation has been served. In the meantime, my work will continue on your behalf from the Elite city. It was great meeting you, Claire, and I wish us both the best."

"Nice to meet you too," I force myself to say.

With that, she leaves me alone with Mr. Smith. I turn my attention to him, seeing subtle movement pass over his head.

He seems to catch sight of the roving camera out of the corner of his eye, a look of distaste pulling the corners of his lips. "Now that that's settled," he says, "we have your secondary sentence."

My stomach drops. "Secondary?"

"Like Ms. Wan said, being a Reality candidate doesn't guarantee you'll get a show of your own, which makes it a light sentence in ratio to your debt. Most probationary sentences that involve being a candidate for Reality viewing require a secondary sentence."

I nod, unable to speak.

He looks at the flat panel of his computer screen. "You will serve as a subject for psychological study for Dr. Geraldine Shelia."

My mind spins, trying to make sense of his words. Psychological study. Is that...experimentation? Drug testing? "What does that mean?"

Mr. Smith's face goes soft, showing a hint of sympathy. "It's nothing to worry about. Honestly, I think you got off easy here too. The judges probably read your file, and seeing what happened to your mother and father, probably thought time with a psychiatrist would be good for you."

"So it isn't..." My eyes are wide, and I can't bring myself to finish my sentence.

"It isn't anything harmful, if that's what you're thinking. You meet with Dr. Shelia tomorrow, and every Wednesday to follow, for an hour."

My relief is mingled with disappointment. An hour spent each week with Dr. Shelia means an hour spent not working. An hour *not* dedicated to my eventual freedom from probation.

Mr. Smith slides a rectangular metal badge across his desk. "This is your pass into the Select District, for work use and your appointments with Dr. Shelia only. It will also provide access to the four city buildings you have clearance to enter: Salish Diner, Great Northwest Hotel, Four Corners Bistro, and the Select Health and Disease Prevention building. This," he passes me another badge, this one plastic, "is the key to your apartment. Further information has been sent to your reader."

I reach for the badges and tuck them into the pocket of my jacket.

He rises to his feet, and I rise to mine. "Good luck, Claire Harper." I move to the door. My fingers touch the handle, but before I can turn it, he speaks again, his words coming out fast, as if he needs to say them before he can stop himself. "I'm sorry for what happened to your parents."

I look back at him, surprised.

"I have a daughter almost your age," is all he says before he returns to his seat, eyes back on his computer screen.

"Thank you," I whisper, too quiet for him to hear, and leave the room.

CHAPTER THREE

The sky is dark by the time I exit the building. After the anxiety I felt all day waiting to hear my sentence, I'm left with nothing but bone-crushing exhaustion. Other than that, I can't tell if I feel relief or fear or sadness. I'm just numb.

I walk down the streets leading away from the Public Citizen Probation building toward the heart of the Public District before I realize I'm not sure where I'm going. Since Mom died, I've been staying in a temporary group home for citizens like me—uprooted, demoted, awaiting probationary sentencing. Now that I've received what I need to move forward, I won't be returning there. I have an assigned apartment now, and everything I own—nothing more than clothes in a backpack—will have been transferred there already.

I stop at the corner of the next street and pull out my reader. It's old and dented, with a few scratches over the screen. Heavy too, compared to the lightweight readers and hologram-based devices I used when I was a Select and Elite. But as a Public, this is what I'm allowed. The screen illuminates with its garish glow, revealing only a few icons—one for approved files, another for communication, a calendar, a clock. The memory has been wiped since I became a probationary citizen, so I know the communication icon will be empty of all contacts. Not that it had many in it before.

I pull up the files and see one for each of my new jobs and one with my housing information. I open that one, studying the address, clicking on it to open a map.

My new apartment is in the Fourth Public Housing Center, building seven. The walk there takes almost an hour. By the time I reach building seven, the streets have gone quiet. Curfew is looming ahead, and no one wants to cut it close if they can help it. I know I don't. Especially now that I've been stripped of my rights as a citizen.

I pull out my reader to remind myself of the floor and room number, then make my way up three flights of stairs to room 86. With a swipe of my keycard over the panel above the handle, the door pops open. Inside, it's pitch-black. Dank odors flood my nostrils, making me gag. I breathe through my mouth, coughing as I move my hand over the nearest wall, searching for a light panel. A dim light illuminates the corner of the room, adding a buzzing sound to aggravate my already overwhelmed senses.

I close the door behind me and rush to the window at the other side of the room to open it. It only swings outward an inch, but any air is better than the stagnant odor I'm breathing now. I turn back to take in my surroundings. My apartment can be crossed in no more than three strides from wall to wall. On one side of the room is a desk, a heating plate, a miniature fridge, and a mirror. On the other side is a narrow bed with simple, brown blankets and a stiff-looking pillow. No bathroom. No shower. The facilities must be communal then.

I move to the desk and find my backpack underneath. My throat constricts as I reach for it, and I hug it tight to my chest as if this one piece of my past can link me to all that I've lost. All that I'll never have again.

I expect tears to come, but they don't. There's still nothing but that unsettling numbness.

With a sigh, I set the backpack on top of the desk. As I do, I glimpse myself in the mirror, which gives me a startle. Looking back at me is a face with dull, pale skin, cheeks and nose flushed pink from walking outside. My blue eyes are bloodshot with dark purple circles hanging underneath. Wisps of my pale blonde hair have escaped my ponytail, leaving a halo of frizz around my head. I look awful. Like a walking corpse.

I bark a laugh—a reaction that startles me almost as much as my appearance—then turn away from the mirror and bring my backpack to the bed instead. Springs creak beneath my thighs as I sit and unpack my things: two pairs of faded jeans, a few pairs of socks, plain loose t-shirts, a hooded sweatshirt, and a pair of worn sneakers. The inventory takes a disappointingly short amount of time, and I put my clothes in one of the desk drawers.

The light flickers, reminding me that the electricity will go off an hour after curfew. Only in the coldest months does it stay on all day, and even then, it's only for some meager heat. It's the end of summer now, so I'm not worried about the cold. Still, with curfew approaching, I should find the bathroom facilities before it's too late.

When I finish my thorough search of building seven, locating all the bathrooms, showers, and exits, I return to my room and pull up my calendar on my reader. Work doesn't start until Thursday, so I'll have tomorrow morning off until my meeting with Dr. Shelia. My stomach churns at the thought.

I've never met with a psychiatrist, so I'm not sure what to expect. I hope Mr. Smith was right. I hope she can help me. Because if I am to survive the next four-to-six years working off my probation, it might be nice to do it while feeling anything other than this numbness. Or the pain lurking beneath it.

I'm not sure how long I've been staring mindlessly at the opposite wall when the light dims, then goes out. I kick off my boots, peel off my jeans and shirt, then lay back on my bed and pull the covers over me. Exhaustion tugs at my body, dragging my bones deep into the recesses of the mattress. Still, no matter how tired I am, I can't seem to close my eyes.

CHAPTER FOUR

The sound of footsteps pounding past my door wakes me from sleep—if you can call it that. It was more like an hour or two of drifting lightly in and out of consciousness. I haven't slept a full night since Mom died. I suppose that's normal. When my dad died, I cried myself to sleep every night for at least a month, and sleep was fitful at best.

Footsteps continue to stream past my door, the sound of Public citizens starting their day, going to their assigned jobs. I wonder how many are on probation like me. How many have similar sentences as mine. How many have invisible cameras circling them at all hours of the day. I freeze, realizing this is the first time I've thought about the cameras since leaving my probation officer. I haven't caught a glimpse of one since then to remind me of them. My eyes dart around me, trying to spot one. Nothing.

I pull myself from bed and check the clock on my reader. Anxiety tickles my chest as I wonder what to do with myself until my appointment with Dr. Shelia. At age seventeen, I'd normally be at school. Now that I'm emancipated, my education is over. I almost wish I'd been assigned to start work first thing, instead of having today off. Even so, I suppose it's best I make use of it.

It doesn't take me long to shower and get ready, throwing my hair back into a messy bun before slipping my sneakers on. Outside my room, building seven looks nearly as dim as it did in the dark. Dozens and dozens of floors—thirty, if I'm counting correctly—reach high above me, blocking the light of the rising sun, creating a semicircle of gray walls and tiny windows surrounding a bare cement courtyard. I leave through the nearest stairwell and find myself amongst several similar buildings that make up the Fourth Public Housing Center.

Once on the main street, I can see clusters of buildings that make up the other housing centers nearby. My eyes catch a familiar building toward the west, and I avert my gaze. That will be the Second Public Housing Center. Where I lived with my mom for the last two years.

After a few turns, I find what I'm looking for—a grocery store. I hate to buy anything I don't need, since I know every credit I spend just gets added to my pile of debt. However, I can't deny that I need to eat.

I buy a meager selection of groceries and take the long way back to my building, exploring my new neighborhood. There isn't much to see. A couple grocery stores. A rundown diner. An abandoned laundromat. A few crumbling buildings that no longer serve a purpose here in the Public District, remnants of an earlier time.

It makes me wonder what Seattle was like before the war. We never learned much about our country's history before World War Three in school. We were mostly taught how our early forefathers suffered, how they gathered survivors from the decimated lands that we now call the outlands and created new societies in the cities that remained intact. We learned how the wealthy Elites generously saved and provided for those who couldn't take care of themselves.

The Elites are the reason I—or any Public citizen—even have a home. Or so I've been told my entire life. They are the ones who donate a portion of their income to the Tithe, which in turn is offered to anyone in need of financial assistance. What I wasn't taught growing up was how suddenly you can find yourself in need of the Tithe. Or how quickly you can become buried beneath its weight.

When I return to my room, my stomach is growling. I pour water in a pot I find in one of the desk drawers and warm it over the heating plate, then use the boiling liquid to reconstitute the noodles I've bought. Without tasting it, I devour the bland meal, then find myself growing anxious yet again. I still have hours until my meeting with Dr. Shelia.

With nothing else to do, I decide to leave for the Select District early. It's been two years since I've lived there, so it wouldn't be a bad idea to acquaint myself with the rail stops and locations of all my jobs. Since I have more than enough time on my hands, I walk to the edge of the Public District instead of taking the bus, then scan my badge to access the rail platform. Once onboard the long, sleek railcar, the Select city comes into view, like it did from the elevator yesterday. This time, the sun is high in the sky, turning the city into a shimmering summer oasis.

I sigh, remembering what it was like to live there. Clean homes. Open spaces. Fresh water. Private bathrooms.

My mom.

My dad.

I jolt upright as the rail comes to a stop, then make my way out the doors to the platform. Scanning my badge as I exit the station, I'm met with the bright lights of the city. The Select District doesn't have nearly as strict rations for electricity as the Public District, so streetlights, signs, and advertisements assault my senses at every turn. The buses here are fast and elegant, nothing like the slow, bulky vehicles in the Public District. And here there are cars, weaving around the buses, zooming past the sidewalks. Bodies brush by, jostling me, and not one set of eyes glances my way. It's loud. It's busy. It's chaotic. And I love it. The Select city makes me feel like I'm home. It makes me feel slightly better than numb.

I follow the map on my reader, locating each place of interest. The Salish Diner on Sixth and Stewart, the Great Northwest Hotel a few blocks over on Eighth, Four Corners Bistro up the hill on Fifteenth and Pine. All are within walking distance or a short bus ride for days when I'm scheduled back-to-back. I hope I'm scheduled back-to-back. The more I work, the more I earn. The more I earn, the faster I serve my probation. The sooner this is all over.

After I locate all my new places of employment, I head to the Select Health and Disease Prevention building for my meeting with Dr. Shelia. I'm an hour early when I arrive, but I make my way inside anyway. The building is immense and brightly lit, with glossy floors and white walls. Everything about it says clean and safe to me, simply for its contrast with even the nicest buildings in the Public District.

I make my way to the oversized hologram near the elevators where the directory is projected. There I find Dr. Shelia's name along with her floor and room number. I ride the elevator to the twentieth floor, then find room fourteen. The door to the clinic is frosted glass, and beyond it I find a bright windowless waiting room with modern-yet-minimal decor.

"Claire Harper?" asks the girl at the front desk. I nod, and she hands me a slim reader to fill out an intake form on. My throat constricts as I enter my personal information. Height.

Weight. Citizenship. Family history. Medical history. Probationary details. The ease I felt from entering the city has been wiped away, replaced with the more familiar anxiety. It grows as I wait, my heart racing as I bite my already chewed-off nails.

"Dr. Shelia will see you now." I look up, finding the girl from the desk standing over me. "Are you ready?"

I nod and follow her out of the waiting room down a short hall. There are only four doors in this hall, and the farthest one down is of frosted glass like the entry to the clinic. My legs feel like jelly as we approach it, and I fear my knees will give out and send me toppling to the floor. The girl stops when she reaches the door. "Go inside. Dr. Shelia will be with you shortly."

I enter the room and hear the door close behind me. My legs still shake, but at least my breathing is growing less ragged as I take in my surroundings. There's a wide, white desk, a chair, and a long, white couch. I take a seat there, shoving my hands beneath my thighs to control their shaking. The walls of the office are bare, aside from the single window at the far end of the room and a few professional certificates. No pictures. No trinkets. It feels clean. Sterile, more like.

A tap sounds on the door, and I can see a misty shadow through the frosted glass. As it opens, an older woman, perhaps in her late fifties, enters. She wears a pair of slim, tan slacks, black leather flats with a Stella Song buckle, and a white blouse. Her clothing style is simple, but there's no mistaking their quality. She's an Elite. I study her face as she takes a seat in the chair at her desk. Her hair is cropped short, a mixture of brown and gray. Her eyes are a pale blue lined with wrinkles. They crinkle even more when she smiles at me, although I can't help but feel that her smile looks forced. "Hello, Claire. It's nice to meet you."

"You too," I lie.

"I've read your files and your intake form. Today's meeting won't take long. It's more to prepare us for our time together." She squints her eyes and studies me. "You've chosen to work three jobs."

She didn't phrase it like a question, but still I say, "Yes."

"Isn't that a little much for your first introduction to the workplace?"

I shake my head and rattle off the same explanation I gave to Mr. Smith. "I'm committed to working off my probation as soon as possible."

"I respect that. But you could still accomplish such a thing while easing into it. Perhaps you could start with one job at a time and add the others once you are used to the first."

I remember my restlessness and anxiety earlier today. "No, that's not necessary. I want to work."

She sighs. "Very well. But if it becomes a problem, I want you to tell me. You may have been assigned to work with me as a probationary sentence, but your privileges are the same as if you were a Select or Elite patient of mine. I am here to advocate for you, if need be."

I'm surprised by this, but I keep quiet.

She squints at me again, and I shift beneath her gaze. "How is your sleep?"

I blanch, opening my mouth to lie, to say it's been great, but there's something about the way she's looking at me that stick the words in my throat.

"You aren't sleeping, are you? That's common in a situation like yours. I imagine you aren't processing your mother's death well." She turns to her desk and presses her thumb over a small metal sensor inlaid in its surface. A keyboard hologram appears beneath her fingers, as well as a projection of a computer screen, and I see her typing something. "I am filling a prescription for you to help you sleep."

A sedative. I'm not sure how I feel about that. It would be nice to sleep for once, but the cost to my credits...

The screen hologram dims, and Dr. Shelia presses a button on her keyboard. "Dr. Grand, we're ready for you." I look around, wondering who she's talking to, but after a few seconds, the door opens. A man with dark brown skin, thinning black hair, and wire-rimmed glasses enters the room, carrying a metal case. He wears black slacks and a white lab coat, fitting for a doctor. Most medical professionals are Elites, but the uncharacteristic wear at the cuffs of his sleeves and the hems of his slacks make it hard to place his rung.

He stops before me and tips his head, like a subtle bow. "Ms. Harper, I'm Dr. Grand." I'm surprised by his formality as well as his blank expression. Even when he smiles, his face still reminds me of an empty canvas. He sets the case next to me on the couch, opening it to reveal two-dozen flat metal disks. My breath catches, remembering what Kori did to my wrist. It's still tender where the metal edges of the tracker meet my flesh. I lean away, watching Dr. Grand with alarm.

His eyes flash to my fingers clutching reflexively around my wrist. As if he understands my worry, he takes a step back and opens his hands, palms forward. "These will do you no harm," he says slowly. It may be his gentle tone or the way his eyes turn down at the corners when he looks at me—the only hint of emotion on his otherwise blank face—but for some reason, I believe him.

I take a deep breath and relax back into my seat while Dr. Grand removes the disks from their case. With bated breath, I feel him place the cold metal in the middle of my forehead, then two others at my temples, and several more over my scalp. They remain in place without latching into my skin, prompting a shaky exhale from my lips. With all the disks in place, Dr. Grand faces a corner of the room where a hologram has illuminated. I glance at it, seeing what looks like an image of a brain. *My* brain. Different colors swirl over the image with rows of numbers, letters, and abbreviations below it, but I don't know what any of it means.

"Your vitals don't look too good, Claire," Dr. Shelia says. "If I didn't already know you weren't sleeping, I'd know now."

Dr. Grand types some information into a reader. When he's finished, he sets the reader down and the hologram disappears.

"We will begin our official work together next week," Dr. Shelia says as Dr. Grand removes the disks from me and replaces them in the case. "In the meantime, I want you to take care of yourself. Take your pills. Emily will have them waiting for you at the front desk when you leave. I want you to get a good night's sleep."

Her tone conveys a clear dismissal, but I still have questions. "How much will the medication cost me?"

She frowns. "Emily will have a total for you at the front desk. You don't need to worry about it. It will be charged to your credits."

That's exactly what I'm worried about. But instead of arguing, I stand and leave her office. As I approach the desk in the waiting room, I consider brushing past it. I can't be charged for a medication I don't claim, right? Before I can ponder it a moment longer, the girl at the desk—Emily—turns and locks eyes with me.

"I have your medication," she says with a smile as she puts a pill bottle on the counter.

I sigh and round the desk to face her. "How much will it cost my credits?"

She eyes the screen in front of her for a moment. "Seven hundred credits."

My mouth falls open. "How long is the supply for?"

"The dosage is for one pill, and there are thirty total."

"Seven hundred credits for a month supply?" I feel like my eyes are going to pop out of my head. I remember my mom's medication being expensive, but hers were more than basic sedatives.

Emily shrugs. "You don't have to take them every night. Only when you have trouble sleeping."

That *is* every night, but I don't say so out loud. I'm about to refuse when movement catches my eye from behind the desk. Dr. Shelia is leaning against the corner of the wall that leads to the corridor, watching me. Her lips hold a smile, but I can't help feeling like I'm being judged, bored into by those cold eyes of hers.

"Fine," I say under my breath.

Emily hands me the pill bottle, and I leave the clinic in a daze. An unsettled feeling creeps into me as I reflect upon my abrupt meeting with Dr. Shelia. I'm not sure what I expected of my first appointment with her, but that wasn't it. It felt so rushed. So...impersonal, despite the meeting revolving around me and my health. Maybe that's what it was supposed to feel like. Like I was being looked at—looked *into*, even—without being truly seen.

By the time I arrive at my apartment, it's almost curfew. I scrape together another unsatisfying meal, then check the calendar on my reader. I'll be starting work at six the next morning, which means I'll need to wake up a couple hours earlier than that. My eyes light on the bottle of pills on my desk, my stomach sinking. I can hear Dr. Shelia's voice in my head. *I want you to get a good night's sleep.* The problem is, I have no idea how these pills work. What if they knock me out so deep, I can't get up in the morning? I can't risk being late on my first day of work.

Maybe I'll try them some other night. Not tonight.

Besides, the less often I take them, the fewer refills I pay for. The fewer credits I accumulate. The sooner I can work off my probation.

What does Dr. Shelia know, anyway? She doesn't know me at all.

I turn off the light and get into bed, staring at the ceiling for another sleepless night.

CHAPTER FIVE

B oth Dr. Shelia and my probation officer were right. Working three jobs is way harder than I thought. What they weren't right about, though, was how much I like it.

It's not that I *enjoy* the work, or the lack of rest, or the physical aches and mental exhaustion that result from it. But I like how it keeps me busy. How it keeps my mind from wandering. It helps me forget the numbness that still lurks inside me, forcing me to focus on the tasks at hand.

On Thursday, it's back-to-back shifts doing dishes at the Four Corners Bistro followed by the same at Salish Diner. The next day, it's laundry at the Great Northwest Hotel. Saturday and Sunday, it's double dishes again. Monday back to laundry. Tuesday, back to double dishes. Wednesday is the only day with any sort of a break, when I do laundry at the hotel for six hours in the morning with a three-hour break before my meeting with Dr. Shelia.

That will be tomorrow. I know I should be glad for the break from the endless physical labor, but I'm not looking forward to meeting with Dr. Shelia again. My stomach sinks just thinking about her bright office, her forced smile, and her abrupt demeanor.

A shoulder rams into mine, bringing me back to my present moment of dirty dishes and soggy hands. My eyes flash from the plate I've been washing too long to the figure next to me.

It's Molly. "Don't get caught slacking off," she snaps in a rushed whisper before moving to the sink next to mine. Molly is one of the other dishwashers at the Salish Diner and works almost all the same shifts as me. While I wouldn't call her my friend, I know her short remarks are made in my favor. She's looking out for me, I can tell. And if anyone knows how a Public can keep a job here, it's her. She's a few inches shorter than me with short brown hair and clever brown eyes. She's rail thin and has one good arm. The other arm ends in a stump beneath the tucked-away sleeve of her uniform. Regardless of this, she still manages to finish a sink full of dishes in half the time I can.

I nod and stack the plate in the sanitizing machine, shaking my previous thoughts from my head. This is why I like work. There's no time to think.

Molly and I work hard through dinner service, neither of us speaking as trays and trays of plates, bowls, silverware, and scraps of half-eaten food are placed by our sinks. Behind us, the chaos of a busy kitchen roars with shouts, searing heat, and mingling aromas. I barely have time to look at the clock as the night wears on.

The Salish Diner is always busy. Being in the heart of the city's tech center, it's often the place for mid-rung Selects to grab lunch on their breaks, then dinner after work before they head home to their apartments in the housing centers. Busy is good for me. Busy keeps me sane.

My hands are raw and red, black uniform drenched in soapy water and bits of food, by the time the dishes start to slow. This is also when my hands start to slow, muscles screaming with every repetitive move, eyelids fluttering, vision swimming over the chocolate-stained dessert plates.

I'm halfway through my final stack when Molly brushes by, already done with hers, of course. "See you Thursday," she says tonelessly.

"See you," I say back. I miss having friends. At least I think I do. I haven't had a true friend since the last time I was a Select. Sure, I've had a few acquaintances over the past couple years as a Public. A boyfriend, even, for a time. Although, I wouldn't call that relationship anything close to serious. It was nothing more than two people looking for a distraction from our miserable lives in the form of heated make out sessions behind our school. There was no point in having anything more serious than that. Not when I'd convinced myself my situation was temporary. *Any day now, Mom will get better,* I remember telling myself. *Any day now, we'll get back to the city. Back to our old life. My old school. My old friends.* I didn't even care about becoming an Elite again. A Select would've been enough.

But Mom didn't get better. Nothing got better.

"Harper," barks a voice behind me, much more aggressive than Molly's had been. I don't need to turn around to know it's my supervisor. I immediately grab another plate and start scrubbing. "I know it's past your bedtime, Public, but that doesn't mean you get to waste water."

"Yes, sir." I force the annoyance from my face. He thinks he's something, calling me *Public* when he can't be more than a first rung Select. I've seen him in his cheap jeans and clearance-rack button-up shirts before he changes into his uniform. He's not the hotshot he thinks he is.

I feel a flicker of flame deep inside, a stirring of something like anger. It almost takes hold, almost grows, and I nearly shiver at the excitement that I'm feeling...*something*. Then just like that, it's gone, forgotten. Back to the dishes. Numbness.

My eyes are burning, both from tiredness and the heat of the kitchen, by the time I make my way to the locker room to change. I toss my uniform—starchy black pants with an elastic waistband and a matching short-sleeved shirt—in the laundry basket before putting on my jeans, loose gray t-shirt, and black leather jacket. My jacket is the only thing I own that I like. It's an older style, but only old enough to be found in a Public thrift store, not so old that it's considered vintage. Vintage is Elite territory.

The streets are beginning to empty as I hurry to catch the last rail of the night. If I don't catch it, I'll never make it back to the Public District by midnight. Midnight is my extended curfew allowance since it's the curfew of the Select District where work keeps me in the city later than the Public curfew of 10 p.m. My allowance is only valid on the days specified according to my work schedule, and any enforcer can find out which days apply by scanning my city badge. I'm not sure what happens to Publics who get stuck in the city overnight, but I know it isn't legal.

I'm panting for breath as I race through the doors of the rail before they close, then sink into an empty seat. Most of the seats are empty since only a rare few Publics are given an allowance extension for work. I look around, wondering if Molly is somewhere nearby or if she caught an earlier route when the rail rolls into motion.

As it speeds along the tracks over the barren land between the Select and Public districts, my body sinks lower and lower in my seat. I dig my nails into my thighs to keep my eyes open. Why does my body only want to sleep when I'm *not* in bed?

Sleep. The word is like a fantasy, and for a moment I wonder what it would be like if I let myself drift off on the rail. Would I sleep long? Would an enforcer wake me? Or would I find myself here in the morning, still in the same position as the rail lurches back into motion for its morning route?

I almost give in and close my eyes. Almost.

The ride is over before my fantasy can linger, and I force my aching legs to stand, force one foot in front of the other and propel myself onto the platform with the other tired citizens. Here, the Public District is black, lit only by the faint light of the cloud-covered moon. I check my reader. Thirty minutes until midnight. Thirty minutes since lights out.

The others have already left the platform and are disappearing into the streets. No one speaks, no one turns and asks where I'm heading, asks if they can walk with me. I've been a Public for two years, yet I still find myself in confused moments like this, where for one split-second I expect to be treated as a Select. It's like I'm a ghost who doesn't know she's dead.

I surge forward, the stress of being out past curfew sending a shock of urgency through me. It was almost this late when I made my way home after my double shifts over the weekend, but the sky had been clearer then, the moon brighter. The darkness less menacing.

The buses don't run past curfew, so it will be a miracle if I can make it home in time. I haven't been stopped by an enforcer since I've been on probation, but I'd rather not find out what it's like. What if there's something wrong with my badge? What if the system hasn't updated my extended curfew allowance yet? I think of the beatings I've witnessed, of enforcers doling out justice with their clubs. Without the rights of citizenship, there's nothing to stop such a thing from happening. I swallow hard and quicken my pace.

I make my way through silent streets, nearly tripping over garbage and debris in my rush to make it home. If I thought my eyes were raw before, they are melting out of my skull as the housing centers come into view. It's even darker here, eerier too, with the apartments rising higher in the sky, blocking more light from the already-hidden moon. I use my reader to light my way, but it doesn't show me more than a few steps ahead.

I get lost trying to find the correct street to building seven and have to check my place on my map in my reader twice before I head the right direction. Something skitters in the street behind me, a rat perhaps, and I pick up my pace yet again. I think I see my building ahead, even though all the apartments look even more alike at night than they do during the day. Another sound falls behind me, a rhythmic beat, like footsteps. I pause and whirl around, but there's nothing to see. *Just another rat*, I try to convince myself. All I hear now is my panting breath and ragged heartbeat.

I continue toward my apartment, almost running, promising myself I'll wash my dishes three times as fast from now on, determined never to be out this late again. I catch that rhythmic sound again—it *has* to be feet. An enforcer? I don't turn around to look, I just keep going.

That's when I see it. Movement. Nothing more than blackness moving through blackness, but it's there, just ahead, on the other side of the street. I slow down and squint into the dark, my heart pounding in my chest as if it might explode. Movement again. I look from side to side, seeking a direction to run.

Then a sound, chilling and strangled, sending a shiver up my spine, breaks the silence of the night. "Claire?"

I could never forget that voice, no matter how quiet, how distant, how nearly imperceptible it is. With shaking hands, I lift my reader, letting the subtle glow fall on the street across from me. There, at the corner, stands a familiar figure.

She looks scared, confused, her face frozen as she waits motionless, staring back at me.

My voice cracks on the word that breaks from my throat. "Mom?"

Without realizing it, I am crossing the street, eager to reach her. In that moment, I see nothing else. Hear nothing else. Not the darkened streets, not the buildings rising around us, not the lights of the bus that barrels my way. I only notice it when I'm on the ground, my arm crushed beneath me, something heavy pinning me down. My breath wheezes out as the weight rolls off me. I watch the bus round the corner, shining its dull lights over where my mother just stood.

I remember the weight that crushed me to the ground and turn, finding a figure scrambling to his feet. I stand too, taking an unsteady step away. He grabs my arm as I stumble over a crushed can, nearly losing my balance.

"Easy," he says as I find my footing. "Are you okay?"

His voice somehow calms me, although I would feel a lot better if I could see his face. Is he an enforcer? But no, enforcers wear helmets. This man is only wearing a hooded jacket. His hand isn't holding a club, just the strap of the backpack slung over his shoulder. "I'm fine," I say and shrug from his grasp.

He lets go of my arm and walks into the street. I realize he's reaching for my reader, the screen still illuminated, just a few inches from the sidewalk. As he hands it to me, I look up, catching a glimpse of his features. I'm taken aback at how young he is. He can't be much older than I am.

I take the reader, but keep it on, the light like a protective barrier between us. "Who are you?"

His brow furrows, then his lips pull into a crooked smile. "No, *thank you, kind soul, for saving my life?*"

He has a point, but I think of the footsteps I heard behind me. "Were you following me?"

"Not intentionally," he says, "but I need to get home before extended curfew just as much as you do, and we're apparently going the same direction."

"Why didn't you just say something instead of creeping along behind me?"

He shrugs. "I didn't want to scare you."

"Well, great job." I cross my arms over my chest, heart continuing to race. A suspicious thought weaves through my consciousness. "How were you behind me? I was the last person to leave the platform, and I didn't see you on the rail."

The crooked smile is back. "Geez, thanks. That makes me feel great. Not only am I a creep, but an utterly forgettable one."

I purse my lips, glaring. "You didn't answer the question."

He sighs. "I saw *you* on the rail. I was sitting behind you, and I was behind you on the platform. Not in a weird way or anything," he rushes to add when I raise my brows. "I was about to ask where you were headed when you took off. Once I realized we were going the same way, it was too late to say anything. I could tell you were already freaked out."

"How could you tell?"

He hunches his shoulders and tosses his head left and right, eyes wide in what must be his imitation of me. I deepen my glare, and he lets out a small laugh. "Hey, it's a good thing I was following you, creep or not, right? Or would you rather I'd let the bus take you down?"

I remember the bus, the shock of finding it mere feet away from me. Another question comes to mind. "What was a bus doing out this late in the first place? It was lights-out well before I got off the rail."

The boy shrugs. "The buses are like railcars. They run on reservoirs of electricity instead of directly from the grid. It was probably going back to base from its last run. Maybe it had some kind of mechanical malfunction that kept it out later than usual."

That reminds me. I look at my reader, seeing it's twenty minutes past midnight.

He must be able to read the anxiety on my face. "Can I walk you home?"

My eyes move back to the boy. The boy with no name. "You never answered my first question. Who are you?"

He reaches out a hand. "Darren. And you are?"

I hesitate before placing my hand in his. "Claire."

We shake hands briefly, then Darren reaches into the pocket of his jacket and pulls out his own reader. The screen illuminates, adding its pale light to mine. "Two is better than one. Where to?"

I never agreed to walk with him, but I have to admit, the idea of walking alone after the fright I just experienced sounds awful. "Fourth Public Housing Center, building seven," I finally confess.

"Same here, but I'm building four," he says. "Come on."

We make our way down the street, toward the corner. *The corner.* Where I saw my mom.

The shock of nearly getting hit by a bus has cleared my mind. Only now do I realize I couldn't have possibly seen her. Couldn't possibly have *heard* her. Still, I shudder as we reach the corner, where nothing but piles of overstuffed black garbage bags lie dormant.

Perhaps my rigid posture is noticeable, because Darren leans toward me and says, "Are you sure you're okay?"

I don't know how to answer that. No, I just hallucinated that I saw my dead mother and nearly died myself? Yes, thank you for saving me? I settle for the truth. "As okay as I can be."

He doesn't press me further, and we walk the rest of the way in silence. When we reach the courtyard of my building, we stop, and Darren faces me. "Do you want me to walk you to your room?" I shake my head, and he smiles, the light of our readers showing something I don't think I've seen from a stranger in a long time. Genuine kindness. "Get home safe, then."

It's that kindness that makes my apprehension drain away, and I'm stumbling over how to respond. I should thank him. I should smile back. Instead, I mutter, "You too," and turn away from him.

I look over the railing when I reach my door, and find his silhouette in the courtyard. He waves, then turns away, heading toward the other apartment buildings.

Once inside my room, I sink to my bed, feeling suddenly weak. The events of the night strike me hard, and my heart starts to race again as I relive my travels through the dark streets, the sounds of muffled footsteps behind me, my mother's face before me. The lights of the bus, just seconds away from impact. Darren, pushing me from its path and crushing me into the sidewalk.

And then I realize...

I was afraid tonight. I *felt* something.

It may have culminated in a jarring hallucination, but it was *something*. A giddy relief winds its way through my stomach, releasing the tension in my gut, my chest, my throat. I recall the way my name sounded, spoken by my imagined mother. *Claire*. With that, I unravel, sobs tearing from my throat like a bird escaping a too-small cage. Tears stream down my cheeks, burning my eyes, searing my skin in trails of heat as I give in to the sorrow that crashes over me like a wave.

I let my grief pour out of me, luxuriating in finally being able to feel, finally being able to process some of the pain I've been hiding.

When my tears dry, I close my eyes.

For the first time in two weeks, I sleep.

CHAPTER SIX

I wake with the strange sensation of feeling both groggy and rested, as if my mind is refreshed but my body—eyes, limbs, muscles—can't reconcile what I'm forcing them to do. Still, I swing my legs over the bed and stand. Memories from last night come rushing back. My terror walking the dark streets. My mom. Darren. It's almost like a dream, and I spend countless minutes second-guessing whether it actually happened.

But it did. I know it did.

With automatic movements, I get ready for my day. Use the facilities. Get dressed. Eat some flavorless oatmeal. Walk to the bus stop. The numbness is back as I go about these routine motions, but it feels tenuous now, like I could summon the fear from last night in an instant if I wanted to. Even waiting for the bus under the full light of the morning sun offers a morbid thrill, sending a prickle up the back of my neck as I see it round the corner.

This time, though, the bus doesn't nearly collide with me and instead stops a safe distance away. I file inside along with the numerous other citizens. As I take my seat in the packed bus, I find myself looking around. But what am I looking for?

Hooded jacket. A smile. That's all I remember about the boy who rescued me last night. And when I don't see anyone resembling him, I feel an unexpected pang of disappointment.

The bus lurches into motion, and I return to the routine of my day. Numbness. Bus. Rail to the city. Laundry at the Great Northwest Hotel.

The scents of bleach and chemical cleaning agents burn my throat as I work, even with the face mask covering my nose and mouth. Unlike at the restaurants, here I am offered thick rubber gloves to do my tasks in, so my hands get a break from the assault of hot water they are used to. Perhaps it's because I know my shift is only six hours long, but I'm working faster today, lighter on my feet. I find myself listening to the conversations of the other women who work the laundry room with me, women I usually ignore.

One of them—Marlene, I think it is—pauses when she catches me laughing at something she said. I'm worried for a moment that I've overstepped some invisible boundary, something that should keep someone like me from engaging with the more seasoned workers, but my worry fades when her lips flick into a smile. "I thought you were mute, new girl," she teases.

My first inclination is to brush off her comment and return to my work without reply, but something else bubbles within me. Something bold and carefree. Something that recognizes her expression as an invitation to participate in some long-forgotten art. "Maybe that's what I wanted you to think."

Marlene barks a laugh as she stuffs a heaping armful of towels into an enormous washing machine. "Oh yeah? And why would you want me to think that?"

"Isn't that the best way to know everyone's secrets?" Banter. That's the long-forgotten art. Something I once reserved for my friends when I was a Select. Or for my mom.

"Ha! What would a young thing like you want with the secrets of old birds like us?"

I offer an innocent shrug, keeping my eyes on the stain I'm scrubbing from a white sheet. "I don't know. Maybe I have a thing for old, balding men."

The other women hoot with laughter over the groaning of the machines around us.

Marlene lets out an exaggerated gasp. "Now, who would you be calling old and balding?"

"I've seen Sergio from delivery."

"She's feisty," says another woman, Carol. "Looks like we need to be careful with this one!"

Marlene shakes her head with a scolding glare, but she can't hide her amusement. "You keep your hands off my Sergio. If he falls down a rung, he's mine."

"If you say so." I smile. Our work continues along with the chatter, but this time I'm included, enfolded into the tiny clan of laundry room women. Conversation is light, teasing, never touching on anything serious about our lives or statuses beyond exaggerated lamentations over the woes of our tasks. It's as if our biting remarks, when made in jest, somehow help us forget the very real truths of our humble situations.

It makes me wonder why I never spoke to them before today, or why I barely engaged with Molly at the restaurant. I never thought I was better than any of them—or worse, for that matter. It's just that I didn't...care. About anything.

I'm still riding the strange wave of lightheartedness hours later as I enter Dr. Shelia's clinic. I've almost forgotten my previous trepidation over this meeting, and it only returns as a slight unease when I enter the bright office room and take a seat on the couch.

"Dr. Shelia will be in momentarily," Emily, the receptionist, says before she closes the door and leaves me alone in the room.

I'm less nervous this time, probably because I'm so distracted by my odd mood, but I sit on my hands just the same to keep myself from fidgeting.

Dr. Shelia enters after a few minutes and takes her seat at the desk. "Hello, Claire," she says as she leans back in her chair and eyes me over a pair of narrow glasses. Her voice is gentle, but her smile is cold and forced like last time. "How has your sleep been since I last saw you?"

I open my mouth, but I'm not sure what to say. I settle for the truth. "I slept well last night."

"Is that the only night you've slept well this past week?"

"Yes."

"You haven't taken the pills I've given you." It isn't a question. She knows.

"I haven't." There's no use lying, I suppose. "I was worried how they would interfere with my work performance."

Dr. Shelia sighs, clearly disappointed. Her eyes unfocus for a moment before returning to mine. "What was different about last night that made sleep happen for you? Was it because your schedule was less demanding this morning?"

"No," I say, before realizing I've negated the one excuse that could have allowed me to keep the events of last night to myself. Yet, I can't ignore the strange urging I feel in my gut. I'm not sure why, but I think I *want* to talk about it. And isn't that what Dr. Shelia is here for? For me to talk to?

Without intending to, I narrow my eyes at her as I decide whether I should open up or remain closed off. Numb. Quiet. My norm for the past couple weeks—months, even.

"What is it?" Dr. Shelia says, her expression mirroring mine, eyes boring into me as if she can read my thoughts by looking at my face.

I look away, fixing my gaze on her desk instead.

"You can talk to me, Claire. Why don't you lie down?"

I take in the couch I'm sitting on. It's likely the nicest piece of furniture I've sat on since I've been a Public, with its clean, white, cloth-covered cushions and sturdy construction. Nothing like my narrow, squeaky bed in my apartment. "Here? With my shoes and everything?"

"You can take off your shoes," Dr. Shelia says gently. "But yes, lie down. It might make you more comfortable when talking to me."

I shrug, remove my shoes, then lie back on the couch. As I shift into the cushions beneath me, I learn that the couch isn't nearly as comfortable as it is nice. Maybe it's designed that way to keep me awake. "Okay," I say.

"Now tell me what happened."

I take a deep breath. "I saw my mom last night."

"Your mom." Dr. Shelia's voice is devoid of judgment—or any emotion, for that matter. This surprises me since I know she's read my file. She knows my mom is dead. Still, she says nothing else, just remains quiet.

When I realize she isn't going to prompt me to explain, I continue on my own. "I was on my way home from my double shift at the two restaurants last night. I was tired and jumpy. When I was almost home, I started hearing sounds, like I was being followed." I *was* being followed, by Darren, but I don't mention this just yet. "Then I heard my name, and it sounded like my mother's voice. It sounded so real. Then I saw her. *Thought* I saw her."

"What did she look like?"

"Like she always did, but hazy, because of the dark. She looked scared. Confused."

"What happened next?"

Now it's time to mention Darren and the bus, but I hesitate.

"Take a deep breath," Dr. Shelia prompts. "Relax your muscles."

I've grown tense since I've started talking about last night, as if I'm back on that dark street. I do as she says and breathe deeply until I feel my muscles unclench. Back to numb. No, not numb. More of a neutral curious.

"Go on, Claire."

"I almost got hit by a bus," I finally confess. "I was so fixated on my mom, I didn't see or hear it coming. A man saw me and pushed me out of the way before it could hit me."

"Who was the man?"

"I didn't know him. He'd been walking behind me on his way home but didn't want to scare me by making his presence known before then." I'm not sure why I feel so determined to make it clear Darren wasn't as nefarious as I first thought him to be. It isn't like I know anything about him. Still, I want to change the subject. "When I got up, I realized how crazy it had been for me to even think I'd seen my mom. I still can't believe how entranced I was."

"You were tired," Dr. Shelia says. "Overworked. Frightened. Hallucinations and everything you've described are common symptoms of sleep deprivation."

I nod. "But I slept after."

"Let's go deeper into that. Why do you think you were finally able to sleep last night?"

"I cried last night." My voice comes out weaker than I plan, and I can feel my throat getting tight. "It was the first time I've been able to cry since...since my mom died."

"How did that feel?"

My lips press into a line, fighting me until I allow them to curl into a tight smile. "It felt good."

Dr. Shelia is quiet for a while. "It felt good to actually feel something for a change."

I turn my head, meeting her gaze. "Yes. How do you know?"

She smiles that cold, clinical smile. This time it doesn't bother me. "Insomnia. Apathy. Neurochemical imbalance. All symptoms of depression, and very common after experiencing trauma such as you have."

Trauma. It's the first time anyone has labeled my experience in such a way. Before this, the labels have been related to my social status. *Inherited debt. Probationary citizen. Lucky you're a minor.* Dr. Shelia is the first person to see my mom's death as something other than an inconvenience to society. A wave of relief washes over me, and I feel like I might cry again.

"Let it out, Claire."

I do. I cry until my body is wracked with sobs, until it feels drained, empty of all pain, all emotion. The time that passes is unknown to me, and when the tears leave, I feel like I did this morning. Groggy. Refreshed. Renewed.

Dr. Shelia hands me a tissue, and I blot my cheeks and nose. "You did well today," she says, then turns to her desk. She presses a button on her holographic keyboard and says, "Dr. Grand, we're ready. Will you bring Claire a cup of water when you come in?"

She returns to face me, sees me swaying in my seat as I right myself on the couch. "Are you lightheaded?"

"A little."

She stands as Dr. Grand enters, then moves to the far end of the room to the window. There she opens it a few inches, filling the room with a mild breeze. I close my eyes, letting the fresh air fill my lungs.

"Nice to see you again, Ms. Harper," Dr. Grand says.

I open my eyes to meet his empty expression. He hands me a paper cup of water, which I drain in a single gulp.

Dr. Shelia returns to her chair. "You need to drink more water, Claire. You're dehydrated."

I nod, and Dr. Grand begins attaching the metal disks to my forehead and scalp like last time. When the projection illuminates with images of my brain, I squint, trying to see if I can decipher anything in its swirling colors as well as the codes and numbers beneath it. To me, it looks exactly the same as before. Confusing.

"Your vitals look a little better today," Dr. Shelia says, although her tone makes me think the improvement can't be too great. "But it won't count for much if your sleep continues to be sporadic and unpredictable. I want you to start taking the sedative I provided you last week. I'm also filling a prescription for an antidepressant." She turns to type on her keyboard as Dr. Grand removes the disks from me. After he replaces them into the case, he sweeps from the room without another word.

I chew on my lip, watching Dr. Shelia typing. "Is the anti-depressant necessary?"

Dr. Shelia pauses and looks at me but doesn't say anything.

"It's just...I can't afford these medications. Besides, I don't want them interfering with my ability to work. I've never been medicated, so—"

"Claire, your health and well-being are more important than your ability to work three jobs."

"But...but I need to work. I need to work off my probation as soon as possible."

She leans forward, holding my gaze. "I understand how badly you want to leave your probation behind, but you won't live to enjoy the results if your body and brain deteriorate in the process."

I stare back at her, not sure how to respond.

"You know I'm right. If you work yourself to the bone, you won't survive probation. It's happened before to citizens older and more seasoned than you. As your psychiatrist, I can't let that happen."

Again, she's speaking to me like I'm more than my status. Like my life might be more important than the debt I owe. But I'm a Public citizen. No. A *probationary* citizen. I don't have the luxury to think like that. I've grown up knowing this. Public citizens are a drain on society. Probationaries aren't citizens at all. The longer I remain one, the longer I let my mom's sacrifice go without purpose.

Rise up, my sweet one. You are worth more than this.

My mom didn't let herself die so I could spend the rest of my life slowly working off the price of her illness. She wanted me to rise in the rungs. To be more. To live the life she wanted for me. She thought I was worth that.

I want to say this, but Dr. Shelia speaks first. "Consider what I've said. I'm going to have you take home your medication, regardless of whether you decide to take it. I want you to think about keeping only one job." I open my mouth to argue, but she holds up a hand to quiet me. "At least until your mental health has significantly improved. After that, you can build back up to the amount of work you can handle."

My shoulders slump. *I feel fine,* I want to say. *I don't care what those brain images show, I know I can do this.* But those words would be lies. I'm not fine, and I know it. I hallucinated last night and nearly got myself killed or seriously injured at best.

"Don't forget what I told you, Claire. I'm your advocate. If you decide to quit any of your jobs, you can tell me and I will dissolve your contracts on your behalf. As your psychiatrist, I have that power, considering your mental and physical state, not to mention your age. You won't be penalized for quitting."

I may not be penalized, but I'll extend my probation. That's penalty enough. However, I don't have the energy to argue my point. My point is weak next to Dr. Shelia's conviction.

I leave her office with a promise that I'll consider what she said. The new medication is stuffed in my backpack, it's eight hundred credit price tag feeling like a lead weight. Anxiety tickles my chest as I ride the rail home, Dr. Shelia's words echoing in my head.

If you work yourself to the bone, you won't survive probation.
You won't survive probation.
You won't survive.

CHAPTER SEVEN

D r. Shelia's warning continues to haunt me as I step off the rail and onto the platform in the Public District. My mind clears quickly when I nearly collide with an enforcer.

"Badge," he says through his black helmet, extending a gloved hand toward me.

I blink back at him, suddenly immobile. It isn't my first time meeting an enforcer. They patrol every district day and night, although the Public District hosts more enforcers than any other. However, this is the first time I've been stopped by one since receiving my clearance to enter the Select District for work.

"Badge," he says again, his voice thick with irritation.

This snaps me out of my stupor, and I fumble in my pockets, searching for my city badge. My hands tremble as I hand it to him. He passes it back and forth over the scanner on his wrist, and I hold my breath, waiting what feels like an eternity for the green light I hope will come. If it isn't green, it's red. If it's red...

The scanner flashes green for a split-second along with a short beep. I let out a sigh of relief as he hands me my badge. At least now I know my city clearance has been updated. Without another word, the enforcer pushes my shoulder, allowing me to file past as he moves on to the next person.

I feel lighter on my feet as I move on, my earlier conversation with Dr. Shelia forgotten. The sun is nearly past the horizon, giving off just enough light for me to traverse the busy streets with ease. Curfew is over an hour away, so I walk without hurry, without fear.

I'm halfway to the housing centers when I sense someone near me, much nearer than what commonly constitutes as proper space between two strangers walking home. I turn, readying a glare, and see a vaguely familiar grin. It's him. Darren.

"Hi," he says.

"Following me again?"

"I said hi this time!"

I roll my eyes, but I'm not annoyed. Not really. "For someone who's trying to convince me he isn't a creep, you aren't doing the best job."

"How so?"

I turn my head toward him, taking in his appearance now that I can see him clearly. The hood of his dark green jacket is down, revealing a head of dark, curly hair that seems overlong in places. His eyes are a dark gray, framed by long lashes and a spattering of freckles over his nose and upper cheeks. His skin is a dark caramel, a color that makes me think of fall leaves and soil and all the earthly things I rarely see in the districts. Things you'd only see in the outlands. He's smiling at me with the crooked smile I remember from last night. It's a struggle to keep my face from mirroring his.

"First of all," I say with narrowed eyes, "you could stop sneaking up behind me."

"It isn't my fault you've been ahead of me twice now," he says. "I saw you on the rail again."

"Why didn't you approach me then?"

"I got held up by the enforcer, like everyone else. By the time I was free, you were nowhere in sight. How do you move so fast on those short little legs?"

I realize he does seem to be struggling to keep up with my pace, even though he's significantly taller than me. But I've always been a fast walker. "So, what? Did you jog after me or something?"

He grins. "Pretty much."

"Why?" I don't know why I keep snapping at him. In all honesty, I'm amused by his presence. Maybe my banter with the laundry women has stayed with me. Then again...didn't this bold and feisty mood start last night with him?

Darren considers my question, brow furrowed as if he's equally perplexed. He shrugs. "After last night, I wanted to see if you're okay."

I raise an eyebrow. "That was worth running across town for?"

"Well, yeah," he says, eyes locking on mine. I feel a blush creep up my cheeks. He returns his gaze ahead. "Besides, I didn't *run*. Running would be stalkerish. It was more of a light jog. Or a fast walk."

I can't help but laugh. "Fast-walking after a girl is *less* stalkerish?"

He joins my laughter. "I'm not selling this whole I'm not a creep thing, am I?"

"No, but I admire the effort."

"Good. Can I walk you home?"

I want to retort that we're already walking, or something else equally as sassy, but I stop myself. Now that we've broken the ice, I find I no longer need the shell of witty banter between us.

I slow my pace as we continue our way home. Not too slow, however, so we don't attract the attention of enforcers. The Public District is not a place for a leisurely stroll. It is a place for going to and from your assigned places of business—work, home, shopping for necessities, or other approved activities. As long as Darren and I don't look like we're having too much fun, we'll be fine.

He tells me about himself. His story sounds a lot like mine; he's a probationary citizen, his parents died and left him with inherited debt. However, his parents died when he was young, and he grew up in the foster system, living in group homes until he came of age at eighteen. He's nineteen now and has been working off his probation for a little over a year. He works two jobs in the city—janitorial at two different tech buildings—and serves as a test subject for pharmaceuticals.

My eyes go wide when he tells me this. I always thought being a test subject would be one of the most terrifying probationary sentences to have. "What kind of pharmaceuticals do they test on you?"

"I think I got lucky. I've been testing a couple different antidepressants, which I probably need anyway, and only have to meet with a group of chemists twice a month to have the results analyzed. Other people with similar sentences don't have it nearly as easy as I do." He pales a little, some of his easy humor draining from his face.

"It makes me feel like I have it easy too," I say. I tell him about Dr. Shelia, our two meetings so far, the medications I've been prescribed, and the fears she voiced concerning my well-being.

"Last night was the first night you've slept in two weeks?" Darren looks at me as if I have two heads. "I can't imagine what that would be like. Some days, sleep is the only thing I like about my life."

I frown, surprised to hear the bitter edge in his voice. With his casual demeanor and kind smile, it's hard to imagine him being an even remotely unhappy person. *Maybe those antidepressants work,* I think to myself. It makes me wonder if I should try the ones Dr. Shelia prescribed for me after all.

"So, what are you going to do?" Darren asks, shaking me from my thoughts. "About sleep? Are you going to do what the doc says and quit some of your jobs?"

I sigh. "I don't know. This has been my plan, ever since I realized my mom was dying. I vowed to work every day, all day if I could, until my probation was paid off. After that, I'll move up in the rungs until I return to Select status."

"Then what?"

"What do you mean?"

"What will you do once you're a Select again?"

The question catches me so off guard, I find myself speechless. I never thought to consider what I wanted to do after I was a Select, only that I wanted to become one again. Rise up. That's my only goal. Become better than this.

Darren can see through my silence. "Shouldn't you have a reason to work yourself so hard, not just a plan?"

"Well, what's your reason?" I ask, my tone defensive.

"That's easy. Work off my probation, start earning *real* credits, save them, cash them out for survival necessities, then move to the outlands."

I pause, my heart quickening. No one talks about the outlands like that. We are all taught in school that the cities are the only safe places to live, that the outlands are toxic from the chemical warfare that ravaged most of the country. The only usable lands outside the cities are the pharms that grow our food, and only farmers and chemists are allowed there. And even under the most careful of circumstances, accidents can happen.

Hazmat suits fail.

People die.

Darren stops and turns toward me when he sees I'm no longer next to him. He throws his head back with a laugh. "I'm just kidding, Claire."

The way he says my name, with so much joy, so much ease, loosens the grip of fear from my chest. "You shouldn't joke about that," I whisper as I return to his side. "There's...something else I should tell you about me."

His brows knit together. "What is it?"

I keep my voice low as we continue walking. "I'm being monitored. My primary active sentence is Reality candidate."

His expression relaxes as he nods his understanding. "I see."

I look up at him, studying his reaction. "Does that make you uncomfortable? Talking to me, I mean?"

He cocks his head. "Why would I feel uncomfortable about that?"

"You know...everything we say, everything we're doing right now...we're being watched."

He lets out a lighthearted laugh. "I doubt that."

"What do you mean?"

"The chances of anyone watching your lifestream right now are very, *very* low. I mean, of all the hundreds of thousand lifestreams and curated shows, would *you* choose to watch this?"

He makes a good point, and I can't help but feel relief that he isn't weirded out by my situation. I'm not sure why I care, but I do.

Darren elbows me with a smile. "Want to know what I really want to do once I work off my probation?"

I'm grateful for the change in subject. "What?"

"Find the right girl. Someone who makes this hellish place worth living in."

I can't tell if he's still teasing or not, but his words make my cheeks feel hot anyway. Luckily, the sun has set far below the buildings of the housing centers by now, so I'm sure he can't tell.

We're almost to my building, and I feel a sense of dread when I think about returning to my room. Alone. When we reach the courtyard of building seven, Darren turns toward me. "You really should consider quitting a job or two."

"Why, so I can spend the next decade-and-a-half working off my probation?"

"There's more to life than working, Claire."

There it is again. My name. I like the sound of it on his lips. "Like what?"

He shrugs, mouth turning up on one side. "Like hanging out with me again."

My pulse quickens and I can feel my blush spreading all over. Still, *hanging out* isn't a luxury Publics have. "Even if I had more free time, what would we even do?"

He leans in close to whisper, "Leave that to me."

I put my hands on my hips. "I'm not going to quit my jobs just to spend time with a boy I hardly know, doing who knows what."

He laughs. "Fine. What's your schedule tomorrow?"

"I work at the Salish Diner until eight."

"I'll be done in the city around then too. Meet you at the rail to ride home together? It isn't following if you know I'm there from the start, right?"

My lips pull into a grin, and I feel a surge of idiotic giddiness. "I suppose you're right."

"Tomorrow it is," he says, then leaves with a wave.

I watch him go, wishing I'd said something in reply. Wishing I could find my wit outside of being sardonic. "Tomorrow it is," I mutter to myself.

CHAPTER EIGHT

It was too much to hope that I'd sleep well two nights in a row. I do manage a couple hours, but my sleep is nowhere near as deep as the night before. However, I have something new to blame. Or *someone*, I should say. Every time I closed my eyes, I saw his face last night. His smile. I would flit between delight and irritation, both enjoying my thoughts of Darren and being annoyed at how persistently they plagued me.

And for what? Why should I let him distract me so? He's no one to me. A stranger.

Still, that smile...

He remains at the forefront of my thoughts as I go about my morning. I look for him on the bus. On the rail. On the busy streets as I walk to the Salish Diner. He's nowhere to be seen, and I scold myself for even looking for him. *He said he'd meet me at the rail tonight,* I remind myself. *If he wanted to see me before, he'd have said so.*

If he wanted to see *me*? Shouldn't he be lucky I agreed to see *him*?

I grumble to myself as I stomp into the locker room at the diner, changing into a clean uniform with more force than necessary. This wasn't part of the plan. I don't have time for boys or distractions. I don't have time for a crush.

A crush. Is that what this is?

I'm grinning like an idiot when I make my way to my sink in the kitchen. I wish I hadn't put my hair in a ponytail so it could instead hide my face, because Molly is staring at me with an odd look.

"Good morning," I say to her, surprised at my cheerful tone. I'd meant it to be flat, empty. Like usual.

"What's up with you?" she asks, looking equally surprised.

I blush. "Nothing."

"Well, don't let it distract you from..." She trails off, her eyes now on my hands. I've already washed five bowls since I stepped up to the sink. She gives me a nod of approval. "Never mind. Glad to see you aren't a spaced-out mope after all."

"Just here to work," I say. Distraction or not, my impatience to see Darren is fueling my pace. Not that working faster will make time go faster, but it does help keep my mind off the passage of time. Luckily, the kitchen is already busy from the breakfast rush, so work quickly overtakes all thought. Since I'm only working a single shift today, I don't even slow down toward the end. The more dishes that pile up, the faster I work. I'm even keeping pace with Molly for once, and at the end of the dinner rush, we finish around the same time.

My eyes flash to the clock as I enter the locker room. 7:23. I'm done early, even for a Thursday, which is my only shift at the Salish where I'm off before Public curfew.

Molly is in her own clothes while I'm still changing out of my uniform. "Want to walk to the rail?"

I'm so surprised, I freeze, arms half-in, half-out of my top. She looks genuine, if not a little impatient. "Sure," I say, then rush to finish getting dressed.

I find she's a fast walker like I am as we make our way down the darkening streets of the city toward the rail. "I thought you were slow," she says.

I look at her, brows furrowed. "Slow?"

She shifts her backpack, settling it more securely over the shoulder of her one arm, smiling wryly. "Yeah. Physically. Mentally. I mean, you barely spoke above a whisper before today."

I frown, realizing the drastic change I've experienced the past few days. It's like my entire existence was blanketed in a fog before...well, before meeting Darren, if I'm being honest. "My mom died recently," I say. I expect my chest to feel tight, for my throat to close. But all I feel is a pinch of grief.

"So, you're new to this life."

I nod. "How long have you been...living this life?"

"You mean being a Public or being a probationary?"

"Both."

She bites her lip, considering. "Well, I'm twenty-three now and I've been a Public since I lost my arm to infection four years ago and wasn't able to work my tech job anymore. I could have continued coding with one arm, but try telling that to my superiors," she says in an undertone. "It didn't take long for me to run out of funds and accept the Tithe. You probably know all about that."

The Tithe. She's right; I know all about that. It's our government's form of assistance for those who struggle financially. Most people with injuries, illnesses, or other forms of debilitating loss tend to require funds from the Tithe. But as soon as you accept even a single credit from the Tithe, you become a Public citizen until it's paid off. The greater your debt-to-income ratio, the farther down the rungs you fall and the less prosperous jobs you qualify for. And once your debt payoff projection exceeds your expected lifetime, you are required to file Forgiveness, making you a probationary citizen until you work off your sentence.

"My mom's illness racked up a lot of debt," I say. "When she died, I was left with all of it. Over two-million credits. Obviously, the payoff projection exceeded my lifetime by far."

She hisses a sharp intake of breath. "That's rough. What's your active sentence?"

"Reality candidate and psychological study."

"Whoa, no shit!" Molly's eyes are wide as she squints at the air around me. "So we have cameras following us?"

I nod.

"I'd say I have to watch my mouth around you from now on, but it's rare for a random citizen's lifestream to get picked up by a producer, much less watched by anyone."

"Really? You mean there's a good chance no one is watching me?" It's basically what Darren told me yesterday, but part of me wondered whether he was just humoring me. Maybe he was right.

"A really good chance. I knew a girl who did coding for one of the Reality channels, and she told me all about it."

I feel a weight fall from my shoulders. It's not like I've given much thought to my role as a Reality candidate, but it feels good to know I might be maintaining some semblance of privacy after all. "What's your sentence?"

Her face falls, then screws into a bitter grimace. "I'm on the draft for the military."

My eyes go wide, taking in her slight frame, her single arm. "The military? Doing what?"

She rolls her eyes. "Probably being bait."

"Don't you have to train or something?"

"I'm sure I will if I'm officially drafted for an assignment. Until then, I wait with my fingers crossed that I work off my probation before that happens."

My mouth hangs open, and I'm once again aware of how lucky I am with my sentence. "That's why you work so hard."

Her face finds its wry smile again. "Five years left!"

Five years. Her debt must not be nearly as great as mine if she only has five years left to pay it off while working one full-time job. Still, I'm amazed by her.

My heart begins to race as I see the rail platform just ahead, and I find myself looking for a familiar smile.

"There's that look again," Molly says. "Spill it. What's really going on?"

My cheeks flush. "I'm supposed to meet someone here."

She raises her brows and elbows me playfully in the side. "A lover? Aren't you too young for that?"

I laugh. "Not a lover. A friend."

"The kind of friend who plasters a stupid smile on your face all day?"

"A boy," I confess. We're on the platform now, and the next rail is due any minute. My heart sinks when I don't see Darren anywhere.

"Don't let me get in the way," she says with a wink. "If he isn't here by the time the rail is ready to leave, I'll go ahead without you."

I see the rail now, rounding the bend in the distance. It feels silly not to catch it when it's right here. No one dawdles on their way back to the Public District. In fact, if an enforcer sees me, he could make me get on. Still, there's a chance Darren meant to catch the next one since I am running earlier than I told him I'd be. "Okay," I finally say.

There's still no sign of Darren as the rail closes its doors, and I see Molly waving from behind one of the windows. As the rail speeds down the tracks, I'm left alone on the platform, wondering if I'm being stupid.

The next rail comes a half-hour later, and there's still no Darren. This time, I don't hesitate to get on. I don't have clearance to be out past Public curfew tonight, and I'm not about to let some boy who can't keep a schedule get me in trouble.

I'm glaring all the way home, feeling wave after wave of disappointment on the rail, on the bus, on the street to my building. Why do I even care? It's not like it was supposed to be a date. Yet, I find myself stomping up the stairs of my building as if I could crush my disappointment with every step. When I enter my room, I swing my backpack onto my bed, then sink into the mattress alongside it.

This is why I don't have time for a crush. It's maddening. It's distracting. I don't like the way I feel right now. But then I remember what Molly said, how she thought I was slow before. I remember the fog that filled my mind the last couple weeks. The way I feel now might be annoying, but it's better than the alternative.

Maybe Darren is a jerk who stood me up. Maybe I'll never see him again. But something about him woke me out of my stupor, and I can't regret that.

After a while, I get up and move to the desk where I rifle through my meager food items. I should have gotten food for dinner with the time I wasted waiting for Darren. When I lift my eyes to check my reader for the time, I catch myself in the mirror. There I am, as haggard as I was the day I entered this room—wisps of stringy blond hair in a frizz around my face, dark bags under my dull, tired eyes. I feel ridiculous for thinking Darren wanted to hang out because he might like me. Why would he like me like *this*?

With a grumble, I turn away from the mirror and check the clock on my reader. There's just enough time for me to make it to the store and back before curfew if I hurry. I grab my backpack and swing open the door.

I freeze. Outside my door, fist raised as if poised to knock, stands Darren.

CHAPTER NINE

At first, I'm stunned, lips threatening to twitch into a surprised grin. His smile comes first, that playful, crooked smirk, and I'm reminded of what it felt like to think about him all day, only to be stood up on the rail platform.

I cross my arms over my chest. "What are you doing here?"

His smile falters, but he lifts a plastic bag, holding it between us. "I brought dinner."

I deepen my glare, refusing to look at the bag. "I didn't agree for you to show up at my room ten minutes before curfew for dinner."

"I know," he says, his tone apologetic. "I thought I'd make it to the platform in time, but my appointment took way longer than it usually does."

"Appointment?"

"Yeah, tonight was my meeting with the chemists I'm assigned to for probation. I thought we'd be done before eight, but I barely made the nine o'clock rail."

His excuse smooths some of my irritation, and I'm starting to smell whatever food he brought with him, making my mouth water. Still, it's nearly curfew. "You can't be here this late. You'll get in trouble going home."

"I have extended curfew clearance," he says, his smile returning. "I have it set for all my workdays since I have to stay late on occasion. I was off early tonight for my appointment."

I stare at him, debating how to respond. Part of me wants to stay angry, send him home, and be done with him. The other part of me feels warm at the thought of him coming to see me, even though our original plans fell through.

His expression softens. "I'm sorry I didn't make it to the rail platform on time. I would never do that intentionally. When I realized I'd be late, I knew I had to find you."

I furrow my brow. "How did you know what room I'm in, anyway?"

He shrugs. "I didn't. I saw you make it to this floor the first night I walked you home, but I didn't see which door you went to. That would have been..."

"Stalkerish?" I can't help but grin.

"Exactly!" He laughs. "This was about to be the third door I knocked on trying to find you. I'll be lucky if one of your neighbors hasn't called an enforcer already."

I sigh and step aside, allowing him to enter my room. "Fine. But don't expect the best accommodations. My room is—"

"Way nicer than mine," he says, eyes roving the walls of my tiny room until they fall on my desk. "Wait, you have a heating plate? And a fridge? No way! I have to heat and store everything in the community kitchen at building four."

"Really?" I never considered my room to be anything but bare and cold. The apartment I lived in with my mom in the Second Public Housing Center was slightly bigger and cleaner than this one.

Darren sets the plastic bag on my desk and begins opening containers, filling my room with rich aromas. I put my backpack on the floor and look over his shoulder, seeing a sandwich cut in half, a somewhat wilted-yet-fragrant salad, and a fluffy bread roll. My eyes go wide. "Is that...Select food?"

He nods and flashes me a conspiratorial grin.

"You brought Select food into the Public District?" I say in a rushed whisper. "How did you even get that?" While Publics are allowed to purchase and consume what food we can afford while working in the Select District, we are not allowed to take any of those purchases home with us. Darren has clearly broken this rule, not to mention buying a meal far greater than a Public would ever spend credits on.

"I have my connections," he says, not bothering to whisper.

I want to argue, to tell him how much trouble he could have gotten in, but I'm too hungry, eyes fixated on the cheese that stretches between the two halves of sandwich he's pulling apart. It's nothing like the fluorescent yellow, plastic-like slices you find at the Public grocery store. This is real cheese, likely made from real milk. Probably milk from a lab-grown cow, but milk nonetheless. After endless days of reconstituted pasta and oats, nothing sounds better.

We sit on my bed, facing each other from opposite ends, savoring the food. It's the best thing I've eaten in months, maybe years. The only thing that could be better than this is Elite food.

After we finish, Darren collects the garbage and packs it back into the plastic bag, then shoves it into his backpack.

"Don't worry, I'll dispose of the evidence," he says as he returns to his seat on my bed.

I find myself stuck in awkward silence, wondering what to say now that we've finished eating. I haven't been alone with a boy since before I broke up with my last boyfriend almost a year ago. Before that, we hardly did anything but make out. We didn't eat dinner together. We didn't hang out alone in my room. Oddly enough, it was easier to be around someone I didn't have any real interest in. With Darren it's...well, I don't know what it is, but it's different.

Sitting across from him, seeing the way his curly hair falls over his eyes, watching the curve of his lips when he smiles, brings to mind the contrast between us. He's bright, smiling, hopeful, kind. I'm sulky, sharp, and fraying at the edges.

My voice comes out small. "Why are you here, Darren?"

He looks startled. "What do you mean?"

"Why do you want to hang out with me?"

He studies me for a moment, and I feel suddenly naked, afraid he'll finally see me clearly. I expect him to peel away in revulsion at any moment. But he doesn't. He smiles. "I don't know. I just do. Haven't you ever been...drawn to someone?"

I shake my head. "Not as a Public. What's the point? Socializing is hardly allowed, and we barely have time to do so when we are. Besides, Publics can't get married or start families. Not without a heavy fine, at least."

He laughs at this. "There's a lot that can happen between two people leading up to marriage and starting a family."

I blush at the images his words conjure, but I say nothing in reply.

He continues, "And just because we have to work harder to get where we want to be, does that mean we shouldn't enjoy life along the way?"

I ponder his words. It *does* feel wrong to enjoy life as a Public. In fact, I'm *afraid* to enjoy my life. I'm afraid if I feel content, I'll stop trying. I'll stop working my way up the rungs. I'll stop trying to reach the goals my mom wanted for me. *Rise up, my sweet one. You are worth more than this.*

I'm afraid I might forget I'm better than this.

Darren moves a few inches closer to me, shaking me from my thoughts. His knee is brushing mine, making my heart race. His eyes burn into me. I want to look away from them, but they feel like a magnet, locking me into their depths. "Claire, I like you. Is that okay?"

My breath catches in my throat. He likes me. With my dull complexion, my sagging shoulders, my frizzy hair. It isn't possible. "Why me?"

"I may not know you that well, but I know you're more than you think you are."

"How do you know?"

He lifts a hand, brushes it against my cheek. I have to force myself not to pull away, clenching my teeth to keep from trembling. "I just know."

We are frozen like that, our eyes locked, his hand on my cheek. I want to lean into his touch, to inch my way forward until my lips meet his, just to know what they feel like. What would he do if I did? I think about giving in to his words, to let myself feel happy, to sink into this moment where he is smiling at me like I'm beautiful, where I'm about to let my heart unfurl and break free from the cage I've locked it in.

We both move toward each other, a nearly imperceptible distance. My eyes lock on his lips.

Then all goes black.

Eleven o'clock. Lights out.

Darren's hand remains on my cheek a few seconds longer, before I feel him pull away. His laughter fills the room, shattering the beautiful tension between us with an equally beautiful sound. "Way to kill the mood, right?"

I find myself laughing with him, reaching in the dark for my reader to give us some light. We find our readers at the same time and meet each other in the middle of my room. I can no longer see him clearly, but I can tell the warmth in his eyes remains as he moves closer to me. Then he utters the last words I want to hear. "I should head home. Let you get some sleep."

I nod. "Thank you for dinner."

"I won't be late next time," he says.

Next time. There's going to be a next time. My heart does a flip at this.

He smiles. "Here, let's swap contacts so I can send you a message if I need to."

I give him my contact code, and he gives me his. Messages cost credits for Publics, so I know I won't be hearing from him much, but it does give me a sense of relief. Of connection. He *wants* to get to know me, to continue whatever it is going on between us.

He likes me.

My room feels empty when he leaves, and I crawl into bed, seeking the warmth that remains from where he was sitting. I'm staring at the black ceiling, replaying the moment when our lips were only inches apart, when something bright steals my attention. I look across the room at my desk where my reader is illuminated. With shuffling feet, I cross the space between my bed and desk and check the screen.

Darren: *Ride to the city together tomorrow? 7am at the bus outside building 1?*

My heart hammers in my chest, and I type my reply without hesitation. *Yes.*

CHAPTER TEN

We ride the bus and rail together the next morning, as well as on the way home in the evening. We talk. Sit next to each other. Smile at each other when it's too loud or too crowded to talk. Walk side by side until work or home makes us part ways. It makes the weekend—when I work my double shifts at the restaurants—all the more awful since our schedules don't line up and I'm not able to see him at all.

At least I have Molly to keep me company at the Salish. It's the only thing that gets me through my early morning shift at the Four Corners Bistro, where I've still yet to make a single friend. Knowing I have Molly to talk to and ride home with in the evening helps take my mind off Darren.

By Sunday, I feel like I'm starving from my lack of him, though I force myself not to let it distract me, and somehow manage to keep up the quick pace of work I began last week. That's when I finally tell Molly about Darren since I feel like I'll explode if I don't hear his name. Talking about him out loud to another person feels equal parts exciting and terrifying. It feels like speaking about him solidifies that he's real. It also makes me feel like I'm going to jinx things if I say too much. But I can't help it.

I don't, however, talk about Darren with the women at the hotel laundry room on Monday. Our camaraderie isn't like mine and Molly's. We banter, berate, and lament. We don't talk about the beautiful stolen moments that make our lives better.

After my laundry shift is over, I rush to the rail platform, nearly bursting with excitement at the prospect of seeing Darren again, but the message I find on my reader crushes me with disappointment. There's a leak in the building he does janitorial work at. He'll be working late to help clean it up. I've never felt my shoulders sink so low. I'm about to shove my reader into the depths of my pocket when another message comes through.

Darren: *What time do you leave tomorrow?*

I respond: *Early. 6 AM.*

I stare at the screen, holding my breath until his response pops up: *I don't work until 9 but I have to see you. I'll ride with you early.*

My smile feels like it will stretch my face in half. He has to see me. *Has* to.

I feel like I'm floating as I make my way home and into my apartment. By the time I crawl into bed, my eyes feel raw, my body aching from my long workdays over the weekend. My one night of delicious sleep happened almost a week ago, and its benefits are long gone. Exhaustion tugs at every corner of my body, and I want to sleep. I do.

But I can't. And I don't.

• • • •

THE NEXT MORNING, AFTER tossing and turning all night, I shuffle from my bed, shivering despite me not feeling cold. In fact, I feel way too warm. And my limbs feel like they've grown twice as heavy overnight. Sleep. I need to sleep. My eyes fall momentarily on the two bottles of pills—both untouched—on my desk. I consider taking the antidepressant, just for the sheer possibility of it boosting my energy, but the thought leaves me as quickly as it came. Today is another double shift of dishes at the restaurants. If there are any weird side-effects, my day is screwed. Besides, I don't feel *that* bad. Not bad enough to take a pill from an eight hundred credit bottle.

I shift to better thoughts as I prepare for my workday. Darren will be waiting for me at the bus today. That alone clears a fraction of my exhaustion, and I quicken my pace as I get dressed and scarf down breakfast.

I'm practically running by the time I leave my apartment and head toward the bus stop. I check my reader, seeing I'm going to be far too early, and slow down. He won't be there if I get there too soon, and I don't want to be caught loitering at the stop by an enforcer.

My heart leaps as I round the corner and see a familiar head of dark, curly hair. Darren is crossing the street from the other apartment buildings toward the bus stop. When we lock eyes, we both freeze and break into smiles at the same time.

I feel like I'm skipping inside, although I try to keep my cool as we close the distance between us and meet at the stop. We pause a few feet away from each other, and I feel a blush creep up my cheeks. No matter how easy it was beginning to feel with him when we last saw each other, I can't help but feel shy upon seeing him again. My mind immediately goes to the kiss we almost had in my room. The memory makes my lips tingle, and my blush creeps higher.

"Hey," he says.

"Hi."

"How was work the last few days?"

I shrug. *Miserable. Boring. All I thought about was you the entire time.* "It was fine. A bit tiring."

He takes a step closer to me, concern drawing his brows together as he studies my face. "Yeah, are you feeling okay? You look terrible."

I lean away and burn him with a glare. "Uh, thanks."

He laughs. "I didn't mean it like that. It's just..." With a tentative hand, he reaches for my chin, turns my face this way and that. "You look paler than usual."

Good. That means he can't see how deeply I'm blushing. In fact, the feeling of his fingers on my face is making me feel lightheaded. "Well, we can't all be blessed with your perfect complexion." Or perfect hair. Perfect eyes. Perfect lips just inches from mine. Damn, how have I not noticed this beautiful man walking the drab streets of the Public District before? How did he ever sit behind me on the bus without me taking notice?

He pulls his hand away, and it takes all my willpower not to grab it and return it to my face. "Have you been sleeping?"

I roll my eyes. "Who are you, Dr. Shelia?"

"I'm serious. I...worry about you."

I smile. "I'm fine."

"Your words may say so, but your eyes are telling me something else."

I avert my gaze from his, suddenly self-conscious about the heavy, dark circles I know are beneath my eyes.

He opens his mouth to say something more, but the bus rolls to a stop along the sidewalk. "Come on," he says. "Let's see if we can get a seat next to each other."

We are at the head of the queue, so we have no trouble finding a pair of open seats toward the back. I scoot into the seat closest to the window, and he sits next to me, his arm a heavy warmth against mine. I'm almost overcome with exhaustion as soon as the bus rolls into motion, as if the act of sitting has reminded my body what it so greatly lacks. My eyes flutter, and without meaning to, my head falls on Darren's shoulder.

I force my eyes open and pull my head upright. Darren brings his lips close to my ear. "Are you sure you're okay? I've never seen you like this."

"This happens sometimes," I say, my words feeling as thick as molasses. "Especially on a rail or bus. My body never wants to sleep when I'm in my bed."

"Maybe you should try mine sometime."

I sit upright, as if I've been electrocuted, and stare at Darren with wide eyes.

He laughs. "That woke you up.

"Did you just...proposition me? On a Public bus? In front of dozens of strangers?" I'm trying to scowl, but I'm so amused that my lips keep slipping into a grin.

"I'm just kidding, Claire."

My grin falters, and I'm surprised by my sudden pang of disappointment. I mean, yeah, his words were a bit brash, but that doesn't mean I don't want the sentiment to be at least partially true.

"I've got more class than that," he says. "We'd use your place, obviously. It's bigger."

The heat is searing my cheeks and I swat him in the arm. "In your dreams! You haven't even kissed me yet." Once the words are out of my mouth, I wish I could swallow them back up. We have yet to establish what exactly we are, or what we want from each other. I know he likes me...but in what way?

His expression takes on a serious quality, and for a moment I'm terrified that I've said the wrong thing. There's still laughter in his eyes, but a steadiness too. His gaze locks with mine. "That can be arranged."

My breaths have grown shallow, and I'm at a loss for what to say. *Oh my God, Claire. Say something. Say something!* A fire of boldness floods my chest, and before I can stop myself I say, "I'd rather our first kiss wasn't arranged. I'd rather it was spontaneous."

Holy shit. I just flirted with him. Like, *obviously*, flirted with him.

He looks at me with such calm, eyes straying to my lips as if I'm the only person there. As if we aren't crammed like sardines on a bus next to grumbling, groaning passengers at the crack of dawn. "What if I arrange for our first kiss to be spontaneous? Does that work for you? I can pencil you in tonight. Say...11:30?"

My heart is doing somersaults, and I'm trying to keep a straight face. I can't. Before I know it, I'm stifling giddy laughter, earning daggers in the form of glares from those nearby. "Stop making me laugh! You're going to get us in trouble."

He doesn't stop. He continues to make me laugh for the entire bus ride, then on the rail to the city as well. It isn't until he leaves me with a wave in front of the Four Corners Bistro that I understand why. As my legs return to their leaden state and exhaustion pulls my bones, I realize he was trying to help me stay awake. It worked. For that glorious time with him by my side, I felt alive. Energized.

Now it's just me. I shiver, feeling that internal cold creeping back in even though I'm dying to shrug out of my leather jacket. It's too warm. Everything feels too warm. What's wrong with me today?

There isn't much time to consider it. What's the point? Work awaits.

CHAPTER ELEVEN

My head feels like a balloon filled with water by the time I make it to the Salish Diner for my evening shift. I'm late. I shouldn't have insisted on walking all the way from the Bistro.

Molly glares at me when I reach the sink, her eyes delivering a warning. "You cut it way too close," she whispers. "You're lucky Mr. Evans has been on break. When he sees your time punch, though, he's gonna be furious."

"I know," I say, and with the words comes a searing pain through my skull. I wince and close my eyes until the pain recedes.

Molly's expression shifts from warning to worry. "What's wrong?"

"I don't know. I just don't feel that well today."

"Are you getting sick?"

"Maybe." I haven't wanted to admit the possibility until now, but the question strikes a chord inside me. Getting sick is a Public's worst nightmare, and it's even worse for a probationary. We can't afford to get sick. We can't afford supplements or doctor visits. And, unlike Selects and Elites, we aren't given paid days off for emergencies, so we can't afford to miss work either.

Worst of all, if I get sick, how am I supposed to kiss Darren? I think to myself, and I nearly laugh out loud at the absurdity. That's my biggest concern right now? Kissing? I'm reminded of how lighthearted I felt with him this morning, and the shadow looming over me begins to dissipate.

Then I deliver the same lie I've told again and again. To Dr. Shelia. To Darren. Now to Molly. "I'm fine. I'll be fine."

My misery grows with every hour, and by the time dinner service begins, I can barely keep my eyes open. For once, it isn't because I'm tired. I am still tired, but more pressing is how the light of the kitchen shoots ripples of excruciating pain through my head. My pace is slow, and I'm not even trying to keep up with Molly anymore. I ignore her stares of concern as she watches me drag my way through my stacks of dishes. I don't argue when she shuffles by and removes an armful of plates from my sink and brings them to hers. I should though. She could get in trouble for lightening my workload.

After the plates, I move on to the wine glasses, scrubbing them with a soft sponge and detergent. I hate how badly my hands shake. Select dishware isn't nearly as delicate as Elite, but I still get nervous when handling the glasses. Anything I break gets charged on my credits. Luckily, I haven't broken anything yet.

I'm on the last glass, sweat beading my brow even though I still feel that inner chill. How much longer can I do this? I lift my eyes to the clock, but the motion sends my head into a spin, and pain shoots through my skull.

I squeeze my eyes.

I squeeze my hands.

There's the sound of shattering glass.

I open my eyes and see soap mingling with streams of red, running over what remains of the fractured wineglass lying at the bottom of the sink. Pain registers in my hand, and I realize the red is coming from me, from a gash slowly widening across my palm. The sight of blood renews the nausea I felt moments before, bringing with it a lightness in my head, a trembling in my knees.

I hear Molly's squeal of alarm as I hit the floor.

• • • •

WHEN I COME TO, MOLLY is leaning over me and a dishrag has been tied over my palm. Another face leans over me as well. It's my supervisor, Mr. Evans. "Can you get up?" he asks with impatience.

I force myself to sit, though each inch that I rise brings greater pain to my skull.

Mr. Evans faces me with his hands on his hips. "Can you work?"

"She needs stitches," Molly says, hand on my shoulder. "And probably other kinds of medical care."

I try to lie, but 'I'm fine,' won't seem to make it past my lips this time.

Molly and Mr. Evans begin to argue, but their words seem suddenly too loud and too quiet at once, drowned out by the beating of my pulse echoing through my head.

I take a deep breath and try to reorient myself. Molly's words come clearly. "I'll take her to the hospital. When I come back I'll do both our dishes. I won't leave until they're done."

Mr. Evans stomps away without answering her.

Without another word, Molly is lifting me, arm around my waist. I try as hard as I can to stand, but the blood feels like it's draining from my head to my toes.

"Come on," Molly says. "The hospital isn't far, and some air will do you good."

"I can't go to the hospital," I mumble.

"You can and you will."

"No. Can't afford it."

Molly faces me, forcing me to meet her eyes. "Can you afford to lose your arm to infection? Because that's what happens to those who refuse medical treatment."

Her words send a chill up my spine. Is that what happened to her? "Not the Select then. I'll take the rail to the Public Hospital."

"Oh yeah? Do you really think they will let you on the rail to bleed all over the other passengers?"

I look at my hand and see the dishtowel has already become soaked in red.

She tugs me forward. "You're going. No more arguing so we can get this over with. I'm the one who has to stay late now."

We make our way to the locker room to grab my things, then out of the restaurant into the streets of the city. Citizens stream past us, either on their way home from work or out to dinner, and no one pays any attention to the one-armed girl dragging her half-conscious friend.

The mild air outside feels good and helps clear my head somewhat. When I'm able to support myself better, I pull my weight off Molly. "I'm sorry," I say. "I don't know what happened."

"Life happened, Claire." Her tone is bitter, but I don't get the feeling it's directed at me. "You worked too hard. You got sick. You worked harder. And now you're paying for it. It's the probationary way."

"You really think I need stitches?"

"Yeah, and more."

I fight to maintain consciousness as we walk, my head still throbbing, sweat coating my face. Once we arrive at the hospital, Molly guides me to the Public wing, a small, dimly lit portion of the building reserved for the few Publics who need medical care while in the city.

Molly checks me in at the front desk, then turns to face me. "I don't care what kind of treatment they will say you need. Accept it. All of it." Her tone is filled with annoyance, but beneath it is something else. Something I recognize from when my mom was fighting for her life the past few years.

She cares about me.

My throat feels tight as I meet her eyes. "Thank you for bringing me here. And I'm so sorry you have to stay late to do my share of the dishes."

"It's fine. Just...get better, okay?" With that, she turns and leaves me alone in the waiting room.

I sit in one of the chairs until a nurse comes to get me. She isn't smiling as she leads me to a room and conducts her initial assessment. The next few hours pass in a blur. I lay on the hospital bed, the room spinning around me. A doctor comes to stitch my wounds. My vitals are taken. An IV is inserted. A needle goes into my arm. Then I'm left alone.

I keep waiting for someone to return and tell me I'm well and it's time for me to leave. It doesn't happen. But whatever they injected me with is kicking in. I give in and close my eyes.

CHAPTER TWELVE

When I wake, disorientation falls over me as I stare up at the room that isn't my room.

I'm at the hospital, I remind myself.

The room is small and cramped with an unpleasant sterile smell. There are no windows, and the lights have been dimmed, leaving most of the room in shadow. If I didn't know any better, I'd be certain I was in the Public District. I suppose I should feel grateful that there's even a place for Publics here at all.

Now that I've received treatment, I realize it was probably the right choice. My mind is clear, the fog lifted, my skull devoid of pain. I lift my hand, finding my limbs still feel heavy, but it's most likely from my nap. My hand has been bandaged, and when I flex it, I feel only the slightest sting. I try not to think about how many credits all of this is costing me, not to mention whatever medications they try to send me home with.

"How do you feel, Claire?"

I nearly jump out of my skin at the sound of the voice and crane my head toward the corner of the room. During my initial assessment of the room, I hadn't noticed the shadowed figure sitting in the chair, and I have to sit upright to see her clearly.

It's Dr. Shelia.

I'm so confused, I blink a few times to be sure my eyes aren't playing tricks on me. "What are you doing here?" It probably isn't the politest thing to say, but it's the most pressing question that comes to mind.

"As a probationary and a minor, you require someone to approve suggested treatment, not to mention check you out. Nearest kin. Guardian."

"But I'm emancipated."

"Not where the hospital's concerned. And since you have no living kin, it was either me or your probation officer."

I'm not sure what to say. Thank you, probably, but for some reason, I'm too embarrassed. If I knew the hospital was going to contact Dr. Shelia, I never would have come here. Besides, she's looking at me with so much disappointment, my cheeks grow warm. "Does that mean I can leave?"

She leans forward in her chair, elbows propped on her knees. "I'm going to have you stay here overnight."

My eyes bulge. "What? Why?"

"Even if you left now, the last rail to the Public District would be long gone by the time you made it to the platform, and I don't—"

I'm already swinging my legs over the side of the bed, eager to catch the rail even if I must run. Dr. Shelia stands at the same moment I remember the IV still in my arm.

"Lay back down, Claire." She says it with such authority, yet her voice isn't unkind.

My head spins from my sudden movement, and I close my eyes for a few seconds before obeying her words.

Dr. Shelia stands at my side, but I refuse to meet her eyes. "I don't want you straining yourself. You only feel as well as you do because you're being medicated. You would have experienced nothing more than a common cold, but cutting your hand, losing blood, and your prolonged neglect of self-care has caused a severe crash in your vitals. I want you to stay overnight until you stabilize."

"But...I can't."

"You don't have many other choices. Publics who are, for whatever reason, stuck in the Select District overnight either stay in the Public wing of the hospital, or at the enforcer precinct."

I blanch at this. Staying at the hospital will certainly cost me a heavy fine in credits, but it can't be worse than being locked in a jail cell overnight, can it? "Will they release me before work tomorrow?"

She narrows her eyes at me. "You aren't going to work tomorrow. I've already made arrangements for you to have the morning off. Tomorrow is Wednesday, so our weekly meeting will remain. What you do before you meet with me is up to you, but I suggest you remain in the city, get some food in you, and find somewhere to relax."

I'm so furious, I feel heat rise to my face. What right does she have changing my work schedule? I squeeze my uninjured hand, nails digging into my palm, to channel my rage and not shout at her. My words come out strained through clenched teeth. "I appreciate what you're trying to do for me, but you know I can't afford not to work. I can't afford to eat in the city. I can't afford to stay here overnight."

"Can you afford to tear open your stitches? Return for multiple treatments to fight infection from lack of care? Can you afford to break another glass? Get even sicker than you already are?"

I hate that her words ring true, but I don't say anything.

Dr. Shelia sighs and turns away from me toward the chair. I close my eyes against angry tears, hoping she's decided to leave.

"Tell me about your mother," she says quietly.

I open my eyes. Through my swimming vision, I see she has pulled up the chair alongside the bed. I feel like we're in her office, she in her chair, me lying on her couch. I realize what she's trying to do, and I want to argue. I want her to leave. But the tears have already begun, and the mention of my mother is threatening to tear a sob from me.

"Or, perhaps, start with your father."

That fills me with dread. I try not to think about him. About what his absence did to us. It's not like it was his fault. He didn't mean to die.

"How about this," Dr. Shelia says. "Talk to me now, and I'll cancel your appointment with me tomorrow. You'll have the full day off to recover. You can return to the Public District as soon as you wake up in the morning."

Does she not realize how badly I hate idle time? Time spent alone with my thoughts? Time spent not working off my probation? But the thought of not having to see her again to-morrow makes me consider the bargain.

She must see the resignation on my face. "Your parents be-came Elites when you were eleven, is this correct?"

I nod.

"How did this come about?"

The question seems so benign, but it bears a heavy burden. The weight of it crushes my chest. I consider answering her question but I'm still so angry with her.

"You can talk to me, Claire. It will make you feel better. How did you become an Elite?"

My words come out almost a whisper. "My mom and dad got promoted."

"What jobs were they in before?"

"My dad was in finance. My mom was in law. They both worked at small tech companies here in the Select District most of my life."

"Where did they get promoted?"

I remember it so clearly. The joy of realizing we were moving up not only a rung but an entire class of citizenship. "Santoro Pharm."

"That must have been prestigious for you."

It was. Santoro Corp is a huge pharmaceutical company. Back then, they were just beginning to expand into pharming when they acquired some of the biggest and most barren plots of land outside Seattle. Their chemists were already famous for numerous breakthroughs, producing crops and slaughter animals that not only withstood the toxicity of the outlands but grew at alarming rates. My parents could hardly believe their luck when their applications were accepted. My dad was hired as Santoro Pharm's Chief Financial Adviser while my mom became their resident lawyer.

"How did it end?"

The end. It's funny she would call it that. It's how I've always considered my father's death. The end of everything. Everything good and stable. Life as I knew it. "There was an accident," I tell her. I'm surprised when my voice doesn't shake, until I realize that terrifying numbness is back, covering my emotions like a shroud. Still, I continue. "Mom and Dad were visiting the pharm for business. Mom was in the fields. Dad was near the buildings. There was an explosion in one of the buildings. My dad died from it."

"How did that affect you?"

"Our income was cut in half. My mom had to work twice as hard. She couldn't keep it up. We fell back down to Select."

Dr. Shelia barely blinks as she watches me. "Then what happened?"

"My mom got sick. Turns out, the explosion produced a toxic gas. Even though she'd been wearing a hazmat suit in the field, it didn't protect her enough. She got lung cancer. No matter what the doctors did, they could only slow its progress. She was able to work less and less. Some days she couldn't get out of bed. We slipped down further and further until we had nothing left. We had to accept the Tithe."

"That's when you became Public citizens."

I nod. "By then, Mom couldn't work at all. We lived off credits, thinking she would get better and be able to work again, use her connections to get back into law. She didn't get better. She got worse and worse, while her treatments got more and more intense."

"And then she stopped accepting treatment."

I can feel the protective numbness slipping away, shattering beneath the ache in my throat. "Eight months ago."

"Why?"

Agony ripples from my head to my toes, but it isn't the physical sort. It's emotional. The kind that comes from devastating truth. "She did it for me."

Dr. Shelia's voice is as soft as a caress. "She knew her death was inevitable. She didn't want you to suffer for her debt."

A sob escapes my lips. "I told her I didn't care. I told her I wanted her to live as long as possible, no matter what the consequences were."

"But she didn't listen, did she?" Dr. Shelia says. "She let herself go so that you could have a chance at a better life. She knew you'd be treated with more leniency if you were still a minor when she died."

"I hated her for it."

"Why?"

My voice sounds so unlike me. More like a dying animal. "Because she loved me too much."

Dr. Shelia leans forward. "You don't believe you were worth her sacrifice."

"I wasn't! I'm not." My chest aches with the truth of my words. "I would have given anything to have her with me longer. But she wanted more for me."

"Is that why you work so hard? You want to prove you were worth her sacrifice?"

I shake my head. "I'll never be worth her sacrifice, but if I can get my probation over with, I'll at least be doing what she wanted me to do. I'll be who she wanted me to be."

"And who did she want you to be?"

I shrug. "Better than this. She wanted me to rise. If I can become a Select again, I know I'll be what she wanted for me."

"You don't want that for yourself?"

For myself? Why does she keep saying things like this, like my wants and comfort mean anything while I'm still a probationary?

"Claire, your mother loved you." I hate the warmth in her tone. I've heard softness from her, gentleness too. But never this warmth. It's too much. "She may have wanted better for you, but she never wanted you to hurt yourself to get there."

You don't know what she wanted, I think to myself. *You don't know anything about her, or me, or anything.*

She continues. "She sacrificed herself for you because, to her, you were worth her life."

"I wasn't."

"But you were. You don't get to decide what her sacrifice was worth. Only she could. She wanted to be at peace, and she wanted you to live a better life than it could have been if she'd extended her suffering."

Suffering. That word breaks me. Tears stream down my face as sobs erupt from my chest. Dr. Shelia is right. My mom was suffering during her final years. She continued her painful, unsuccessful treatments for me. Then she let herself die for me. Everything she did was for me.

"She loved you so much," Dr. Shelia whispers. "If you can't love yourself, you make everything she ever did for you mean nothing."

I cover my face with my hands, only mildly aware of the bandage wrapping my palm. "How? How do I love myself when I'm to blame for her suffering in life and her choice for death?"

"You aren't to blame. She made her own choices. You need to accept that. If you can't love yourself, at least start caring about your body. What would your mother think if she could see you now? If she knew you weren't sleeping? If she could see you working well past your body's threshold?"

My gut takes a dive and I pull my hands from my face. She's right again. My mom wouldn't be proud of any of this. She'd be horrified. I've been pushing myself because I thought it's what she wanted. But I was lying to myself. This isn't what she wanted, and I know it. This is what *I* wanted. To punish myself for how much she loved me.

"If you want to honor your mother's memory, then start loving you the way she loved you," Dr. Shelia says, then leans back in her chair. We fall into silence as my sobs subside and my tears begin to evaporate.

When I find my words again, my mouth is dry. "You really think I should quit some of my jobs?"

Dr. Shelia's face is full of sympathy. "You don't have many choices, at least where your immediate future is concerned. You can't wash dishes with your hand like that."

I open my mouth to argue, to tell her about Molly and her single arm, then think better of it.

"If I had my way," she says, "you'd keep only your laundry job at the hotel, but perhaps add a day or two. I don't want you working more than five days a week. Once you regain your health, you can return to your previous jobs, one at a time, if you desire."

I feel hollow at the thought of giving up on my plan. On what I'd convinced myself was my mom's plan. But this isn't what my mom wanted.

"Okay," I finally say.

Dr. Shelia smiles, relief clear on her face. "You're making the right choice. Would you like me to arrange everything for you?"

I think about turning in my resignation letter to Mr. Evans as well as my supervisor at the Bistro and shudder. Then I think about Molly, my heart sinking when I realize I won't be able to see her at work anymore. She was my first true friend as a Public. But she isn't my only friend. I have Darren too. *Darren!* I consider the hour it must be, and I realize he has no idea where I am. Did he wait for me on the rail platform like I did for him? Is he angry? Worried? The thoughts clear the remnants of sorrow from my head, and I'm suddenly eager to be alone. "Yes, please, I would appreciate you taking care of my resignation if you don't mind."

"I told you, Claire, I'm your advocate."

"Thank you." I pause and consider how best to ask my next question without revealing my desperation. "Do you happen to know where my reader is? There's someone I need to let know I'm okay."

"They likely took it when they checked you in," she says as she stands. "I'll approve your overnight stay on my way out and have someone bring you your things."

I do my best to grin. "I appreciate that."

Dr. Shelia considers me for a few seconds before reaching into her purse. "I know you haven't wanted to take medication before now." She withdraws her hand, and in it are two pill bottles. She places them on the bed next to me. "But now that you are committed to taking better care of yourself, I want you to start taking them. I've had both your prescriptions refilled because I want you to double the original prescribed dosage."

My stomach twists with nausea as I calculate the cost of the refills. However, I'm too emotionally spent to dwell on it for long. I reach a reluctant hand for the bottles. Once within my grasp, I study them. One is the sedative. Blue gel caps. The other is the antidepressant. White.

"Two pills of each, night and day," she says, then moves to the sink to fill a paper cup with water. She hands it to me. "I want you to start taking them tonight."

I look from her to the bottles in my hand. What's the point of avoiding it now? I've already proven I'm a hazard to myself without them. Besides, I have no job the next morning to go to, no reason to fear any side effects. If I have a bad reaction, at least I'm already at the hospital.

I accept the water and down two pills of each.

I don't feel any different as I watch Dr. Shelia leave. As I wait for the nurse to bring me my reader. As I rattle off a message to Darren in response to three of his.

Once the message is sent, I place my reader beside me. A sudden calm falls over me. Is it relief from knowing I was able to contact Darren? The emptiness after having such a deep cry? Or is it the pills?

I don't have time to answer.

Sleep is already taking me.

CHAPTER THIRTEEN

I wake feeling the same way I did last time I got a full night of sleep. Groggy but rested. There's also a lightness in my chest, a feeling that some of the emotional burden I've been carrying around has disappeared. I look around the room and find that the IV has been removed and my backpack and clothes are in a neat pile on the chair that Dr. Shelia sat in last night. My reader is still next to me on the bed.

I reach for it, opening my messages. There's one from Dr. Shelia, saying my resignations from the two restaurants have been confirmed. She also says she's requested an extra shift for me in the hotel laundry room that she's confident I'll be approved for. I try not to calculate how much less I'll be earning from now on.

My remaining messages are from Darren, saying how relieved he is that I'm okay and asking when he can see me again. I tell him I'll be off all day today, and we can meet up when he gets off work. His message comes through before I can put my reader back down.

Darren: *I'll see you tonight. Your place.*

I smile, then close my messages and check the time. It's almost noon. Noon! I must have slept almost twelve hours! My heart hammers in my chest and anxiety floods me before I remind myself I'm not on a schedule. It doesn't matter how late I slept.

I slowly rise from the bed, testing my body's reaction. No pain, no nausea, no headache. I move to the chair and begin to dress myself. As I'm sliding my feet into my sneakers, a nurse enters.

"Good, you're awake," she says in a monotone. "Your psychiatrist requested you be allowed to stay until you wake on your own. How do you feel?"

"I feel great." I'm amazed that it's the truth.

"Your stitches will dissolve once your wound has healed. Are you ready to check out?"

Her words send a sinking to my gut, reminding me of all the credits I'll be charged from my treatment, not to mention my extended stay. Luckily, when I check out, they charge me without telling me my total.

I leave the Public wing of the hospital and make my way back to the city streets. It's strange retracing my steps that I took last night, down the hill, past the Salish. I feel as if it wasn't me, bleeding, staggering, fighting to stay upright. I shudder when I recall the blood pouring out of my hand, the shards of glass in the sink.

I feel a wave of gratitude for whatever medications they pumped me full of at the hospital. Yesterday's illness feels like a dream now.

By the time I return to the Public District, I feel a pinch of exhaustion. Instead of walking home, like I normally would when I'm not on a schedule, I take the bus back to the housing centers. I stop at the corner store by my apartment building and pick up some food. A can of soup. An apple. A bag of carrots. I rarely ever spend credits on produce, but I know it's what my body needs.

My stomach is growling by the time I make it back to my room. Once inside, I attack my food, enjoying the bright flavors and crunch of the produce. The soup is less enjoyable, but it makes me feel comfortably full. By the time I'm finished, I'm tired again.

I lay back on my bed, surprised how much yesterday has taken out of me, even after getting a full night of sleep. Then again, when I was a Select, it would take me days to recover from illness. Why should it be any different now? With a sigh, I close my eyes and think about Darren.

• • • •

IT'S ALMOST CURFEW when I hear a knock at my door. With a blanket over my shoulders, I answer the door, smiling when I see Darren's face.

"I brought dinner again," he says, holding up a plastic bag like last time.

"Good, I'm starved." I stand aside, but he hesitates at my doorway.

"Actually, I had another idea," he says. "How would you feel about some fresh air?"

"What do you mean?" I look beyond him, at the dark apartments rising around us toward the night sky. The late August air feels crisp, but not unpleasant. Still, there isn't anywhere to go outdoors that doesn't violate curfew.

He grins and holds out his hand. "Trust me."

I lift a suspicious brow before slipping on my shoes and putting my hand in his. "Fine. Just don't get me in trouble."

"I wouldn't dream of it." He leads us along the corridor in front of my room, past the other doors, the quiet windows. At the end, there's a staircase. I think he's going to lead us down, but he goes up instead. After a dozen or so flights, I begin to slow, feeling tiredness kicking in again. He pauses, arm steady behind my back as he waits for me to catch my breath. "Maybe this wasn't such a good idea."

"I'm fine." This time it isn't a lie. Besides, I'm too curious now. I want to see where he's taking me. "Let's just take it slow."

We continue up the remaining flights of stairs until we reach the top floor. There, another corridor leads to more rooms. He turns right, opening an unmarked door. I'm surprised when I see yet another staircase, this one of thin, creaking metal. Darren turns toward me, just as I realize where we're going. "You first?"

I climb the stairs. At the top, the roof opens into a flat expanse. A light breeze whips my hair from my face and tugs at the hem of my shirt.

Darren follows up the stairs and stops behind me, pointing at the sky above. "Look."

I tip my head and stare at the black sky dotted with stars. Stars! It's been years since I've taken time to look at the night sky like this instead of out of worry or fear of the looming curfew. But for beauty. Joy. Curiosity. Stars.

He leads me to the center of the roof where he unpacks his backpack, laying out a blanket, our dinner, and two cups. Then he pulls out a bottle of wine, and I gasp.

"Where did you get that?"

"Same place I keep getting our dinner."

My mouth hangs open. "How many credits is this costing you?"

He shrugs. "Nothing."

I cross my arms narrowing my eyes at him. "How is that possible?"

"I told you, I have connections. You aren't my only friend who works at a restaurant."

A sudden pang of jealousy squeezes my chest, and I feel the blood leave my face. So...I'm just a friend? And he has more than me?

Something shifts in his face as he watches me, and he rushes to say, "He's an old friend from one of the group homes I lived in when I was a kid. Mitchell. We've kept in touch over the years. He's a line cook at the Golden Tempest. Turns out, they waste a lot of food there since a lot of it gets returned by visiting Elites."

The Golden Tempest is a restaurant belonging to one of the hotels in the city. I feel a wave of relief that his mystery friend isn't a girl.

"It's table scraps, basically," he continues. "Waste that we're putting to good use."

"You could still get in trouble for accepting it," I say, but I sit on the blanket next to him. What's the use arguing when the food smells so good?

This time he's brought sautéed asparagus, roasted chicken, and mashed potatoes.

"Why would anyone return this?" I say with my mouth full. The flavors put my earlier apple to shame.

"Elites are used to more flavor, so I'm told. Bolder pairings. Richer meats. Is that true?"

I nod. "I can barely remember what Elite food tastes like. But I do remember it being different."

When we finish our meal, Darren opens the wine. I realize the bottle is only half full, the cork haphazardly replaced. He pours the red liquid into a cup and hands it to me. I stare at it, feeling a rush of excitement. I remember stealing sips of wine with my friends when I was a Select, but it was more for the thrill of doing it than for the taste. Now that I'm older, I wonder if I'll like it. I take a sip, feeling a warmth in my gut and a buzzing sensation in my head. The taste is far from pleasant, but the results are delightful.

Darren eyes me over the rim of his cup, his gaze hovering over my bandaged palm. "So...how are you?"

I can tell he's trying not to seem too eager, but his face is tinged with worry. With a deep sigh, I unload my burden. I tell him everything that happened yesterday.

His face looks crestfallen. "I knew you weren't feeling well. I shouldn't have made light of things on our way to the city yesterday. I thought if I could make you laugh and feel better, then maybe you'd actually *be* better."

I'm surprised at his guilt. "What else could you have done?"

He shrugs. "I don't know, talk you into seeing a doctor."

"It wouldn't have mattered. I never would have listened."

"I'm sorry you were hurt."

"I brought it on myself," I say. "I feel like an idiot for not seeing it coming. I thought things couldn't possibly be worse than what happened the night I met you."

"When you almost got hit by the bus?"

I shift uncomfortably, then take another sip of wine. "That's not all that happened that night. I...hallucinated. I thought I saw my mom on the street corner. I thought I heard her voice. That's why I was walking into the street. That's why I didn't see the bus."

Darren watches me without a word, without judgment in his eyes.

I continue. "I slept well that night, remember? After that, things changed inside me. I started talking more to my coworkers. I opened up to you. My mind felt clearer. My emotions returned. I thought that meant I was better. That I was no longer a danger to myself. But I was wrong. My emotional state may have improved. I may have let Molly become my friend, and I may have let myself enjoy my time with you, but I still wasn't taking care of myself physically. It was like I felt I should be punished *more* for finding any sort of happiness as a probationary."

I'm surprised I'm telling him so much. I'm surprised he's listening so raptly. Most of all, I'm surprised that everything I'm admitting to him, I'm admitting to myself for the first time as well. It must be the wine. Regardless, it feels good to say these things.

Darren stands and pulls me to my feet. He cups my face in both hands and locks his eyes with mine. My heart races at the closeness, and I fight my urge to shy away from him. "Claire," he says, his voice rich with tenderness, "you are not your status. It doesn't matter whether you're a probationary or an Elite. You, exactly as you are, deserve happiness." My eyes glaze with tears as his words tear my heart in two.

His next words stitch my heart back together and wrap it in a blanket of warmth. "You deserve love."

I press into him, and his lips find mine as my arms wrap around his waist. I've been kissed before, but not like this. Not like the air is being crushed out of me at the same time as I'm being given new life, renewed by every breath we share. My lips part slightly, and I feel his tongue brush against mine. He tastes like wine, and a chill runs down my spine. One of his hands remains on my face while the other tangles in the hair at the back of my neck.

I pull him tighter against me, my hands exploring the flat, hard surface of his back. Our kisses rise like a wave, growing deeper, more urgent, until they crash and slow, our breathing steadying as our hearts hammer between us. Our lips linger together before we pull away and Darren presses his forehead to mine. I keep my hands on his waist while his fall on my shoulders.

When I finally catch my breath, I find my voice. "You're late."

"Late?"

"Our first kiss was scheduled for last night at 11:30."

"Yeah, well, I stood outside your building all night until I got your message. You have no idea how worried I was."

I pull away just far enough to see if he's serious. "You did?"

He laughs. "It sure didn't help my *I'm not a stalker* cause."

I lean in close again. "That's okay. I like this kiss better."

"How do you know? I could have planned fireworks last night."

I touch my lips lightly to his, feel his sharp intake of breath. "That was fireworks."

CHAPTER FOURTEEN

I'm dizzy with happiness as Darren walks me back to my room. He kisses me goodnight, and I pull him against me as tight as I can until fear of him being caught by an enforcer on his way home prompts me to release him. After he leaves, I fall back on my bed with a heavy sigh, lips tingling. Curfew has come and gone, leaving my room in darkness, but I don't need light to see. Darren's face fills my memories, my senses.

It isn't until the buzz of wine wears off that I remember there's a thing called sleep. This, in turn, reminds me of the pills I'm supposed to take. I never did take my morning dose, as I was in such a rush to leave the hospital and get back home. In the dark, I search inside my backpack until I feel the bottles. I set them on the desk next to the two bottles I already have.

From the fridge, I extract a bottle of water, then take the pills to the window, where I find a sliver of moonlight. I combine the two bottles of sleep aids into one, and do the same with the antidepressants, then toss the empty bottles into my waste bin. With a huge gulp of water, I take two of each pill, then chase them with more water.

Only once they are down my throat do I consider the wine I drank and wonder if there are any ill effects from taking pills with alcohol.

Too late now.

The next morning, I wake to a knock on my door. It's Darren. Before I can open it all the way, his lips are on mine, and I squeal with surprise as he wraps me in his arms.

"I had to see you before work," he says breathlessly, slamming the door behind us.

It's Thursday, and I don't return to the hotel laundry room until Friday, which means I have another day off. I'm still blinking sleep out of my eyes, but I must admit, I couldn't ask for a better way to wake up. "How much time do we have?"

"Like five minutes. The bus will be here in ten."

So we make it the best five minutes of my life.

What follows is the happiest I think I've ever been—a week of kisses, of fingers entwined as we walk down the street, of his arm around me while we ride to the city.

I feel guilty admitting this since my happiest memories should involve my mom or dad, right? But they don't. The last few years with my mom have been misery. And the happiness I felt as a child doesn't hold a candle to this. My childhood happiness was the result of circumstance. I felt safe. I was taken care of. But the happiness I feel with Darren is the result of choice. Of action. Of healing. Of opening up to new potential.

The potential for love.

We don't call it that. Not yet. At this point, it's only been a week since our first kiss.

But I can feel my heart opening for him. Cracking wide and shattering into a million pieces with every kiss, stitching back together with each smile, each touch, each tender word.

I only hope he feels the same way.

• • • •

TRANSITIONING FROM my rigorous schedule with three jobs to working only one job is strange at first. I'm surprised how quickly I get tired, even with my new, less burdensome schedule. Then again, I am still recovering from the incident.

Idle time continues to make me anxious. But I've slept all night every night since I started my medication, and I do feel like the antidepressants help take the edge off my anxiety. Besides, I now have Darren to fill a lot of that idle time.

Today is my first appointment with Dr. Shelia since the night at the hospital. For once I'm looking forward to it. Probably because this is the first time I've taken her advice. When I get to the clinic, I'm exhausted despite my shorter shift in the laundry room this morning. It's strange how my body's signals are stronger now that I'm listening to them.

I take a seat on the couch in Dr. Shelia's office. When she enters, she offers me her cold smile, then sits at her desk chair, studying me over her glasses. "How are you feeling?" she finally asks.

"Better," I say. "I've been taking my medication. My hand doesn't hurt so bad, even when I work."

"How are you feeling about working one job?"

I can't help the wave of anxiety that comes over me. "It still makes me feel uncomfortable that I'm not doing more, but I think it's the right thing to do for now."

"Are you sleeping?"

"Yes."

"Good. Any other improvements?"

All I can think about is Darren, and a smile breaks across my face despite my best efforts to suppress it.

Dr. Shelia's brows twitch, a hint of amusement on her face. "Perhaps something more than an improvement?"

I take a deep breath, then let it out slowly. She already knows so much. There's no point in hiding it.

I tell her about Darren. At least, I tell her the things I feel most comfortable telling her. I don't tell her about the kissing or the smuggled Select food or the rooftop dinners. Instead, I share what it's like having him in my life—my fears, my joys, my worries, my excitement.

When I finish, Dr. Shelia studies me again before saying, "He sounds good for you, Claire. I think it's important that you allow yourself to be vulnerable and loved."

Her words remind me of Darren's. Then I think about his lips again.

She continues. "But don't rely on his love alone. I want you to continue to develop your relationship with yourself."

I nod. "I will."

We change to the subject of my childhood. Dr. Shelia asks me vague questions and I answer her as best I can. It's getting easier to talk to her now. We don't touch on anything nearly as shattering as we did at the hospital, but with every word I say, I feel a bit lighter.

At the end of our appointment, Dr. Grand comes in to take my vitals and Dr. Shelia smiles with approval. I'm finally making progress, she says. Keep doing what I'm doing.

Outside the building, I take out my reader but there's no message from Darren. I'm not sure what time he's off today, but I'm certain I'll see him before bed. He's made the effort to see me at least once a day since our kiss.

I try not to be too disappointed when it's lights out and there's still nothing from Darren. Maybe he forgot his reader at home. Maybe he's saving credits by not messaging me.

I lie in bed, but I know I can't sleep yet. Not until I take my medication. But I don't want to take my medication until I know Darren won't be coming.

I check my reader.

11:15.

11:28.

11:46.

It's almost midnight. He isn't coming.

I drag myself to the desk and shake two pills of each onto its surface.

That's when I hear the quiet knock.

I fling the door open with a smile and find Darren standing outside my door, his head lowered. He doesn't move. "Hey," I say, the smile fading from my lips.

He lifts his head, eyes barely meeting mine. "Hey," he says back, not a single hint of warmth in his tone.

My hands are trembling as I push the door open wider. "Are you...okay? Do you want to come in?"

He nods, but his eyes have moved to the floor. I cross my arms over my chest as if I can squeeze out the sense of dread I feel. This is the end. He's breaking up with me. Or were we even together in the first place? Darren runs his hands through his hair and starts pacing. I back away from him until my knees hit the bed, forcing me to sit.

"Something's happening," he says, voice barely above a whisper.

"What is it?" I croak.

"I don't know. I think someone's after me."

I shake my head to clear it. That wasn't what I was expecting. "After you? Who? Why?"

He stops his pacing, stares at a wall. "I don't know. I feel like I'm being followed."

I study his hunched posture, his tangled hair, his wild eyes. This isn't the man I've gotten to know over the past couple weeks. What could have changed? Then it dawns on me. I keep my voice as even as I ask, "Have you taken your medication today?"

"No," he barks with more force than I expect. "It's doing something to me. Something bad."

"Like what?"

"I don't know. I just don't like it."

I stand, place my hands on his shoulders. He meets my eyes for only a moment. "It's okay, Darren. I'm here."

He takes a step closer to me, eyes on our feet. I feel some of the tension begin to leave his shoulders. "I don't want to be here anymore."

I feel like my chest is going to collapse. Does he mean *here,* as inside my apartment? Or here with me?

With a sigh, he meets my eyes. "Let's run away together."

I'm so caught off guard, I can barely form a word in response. "What?"

He seems excited at the thought. "Yeah. Let's go. We can get out of Seattle, move to the outlands."

The blood leaves my face. "The...outlands?"

He turns away from me and starts pacing again. "We can go. People have snuck out of the city before and made it past the pharms. We could do it too."

I shake my head, mouth open wide. "No one can survive the outlands. They're toxic."

He freezes and looks at me like I'm crazy. "No, Claire. The pharms are toxic. That's how they keep us in here. Sure, we would need hazmat suits to get past the pharms, but I know where we can get some without anyone finding out."

His words make no sense. Everyone knows the war ravaged most of the country, leaving behind poisoned land. The pharms are the reason we have food to eat. They aren't toxic. They simply thrive despite the toxicity.

I hear a light buzz near my ear, and I nearly jump out of my skin. My blood goes cold as I think about the cameras. What will happen to Darren if someone is watching us right now? Everything he's saying about the outlands could get him in serious trouble. Probably me too. I know the likelihood that someone is watching my lifestream is slim, but...what if?

I need to change the subject. "Why do you want to leave, Darren? Did something happen?"

His expression is bewildered as he spreads his arms out wide. "Of course something happened! All of *this* happened. The Public District. Probation. This place is *horrible*, Claire." His every word is punctured with rage. Even my name sounds laced with venom.

This conversation isn't getting any safer. I take a step toward him, my voice pleading. "It doesn't have to be like this forever. We can move up the ranks. We can—"

"And do what? Become Selects? Elites? Rise higher and higher in a society that has turned every good thing about our country into a cage?"

I want to tell him to keep his voice down. To remind him about the cameras. But the passion in his voice chills me to the bone. It's like he knows something I don't. "What do you mean?" I whisper.

"It's all bullshit," he says. Luckily his voice has lowered to meet mine. "The Tithe. Forgiveness. Do you know what *tithe* used to mean?"

I shake my head.

"Long before the war, a tithe was something given and received freely. People gave to organizations they respected. These funds were given back to important causes or people in need."

"That sounds like the Tithe as we know it."

"No, it isn't. People tithed *unconditionally*. People received funds from a tithe *unconditionally*. They weren't punished."

I remember what I learned in history. Things used to be the way he says, right after the war. The wealthy saved those in need by giving a portion of what they had. But there were too many people in need. Too many people living off these funds without the ability to give back. Our society almost collapsed. That's when we were structured into three classes and a system of rungs were put into place. Not only did it make those on the receiving end of the Tithe give back to society, it gave them a goal, a clear path to move toward.

But even as I remember this, it contrasts with how I feel now. Stuck. Small. Overworked. I shake these thoughts from my head and return my attention to Darren.

He clenches and unclenches his fists, eyes unfocused. "Why do they call it filing Forgiveness if they aren't forgiving anything? Forgiveness means letting go. A clean slate. Never in the history of the word does forgiveness mean holding a grudge. Not until now where we are punished for choices we rarely have control over."

I shrug. "At least filing Forgiveness reduces what we owe."

"It reduces what we owe," he echoes with a cold laugh. "We owe so much because we are allowed so little. We can't get better jobs until we pay off our debts and rise in the rungs. We can't pay off our debts until we get better jobs. Don't you see? It's a cycle. It keeps us stuck. That's where they want us to be."

His words are bitter, but the rage seems to have dissipated completely. I take his hand in mine and give it a squeeze. "It isn't impossible. We can get out of it."

He looks at me, his face softening. "You're right. We can get out."

Relief washes over me.

"We can leave. We can go to the outlands."

And we're back to treasonous talk of the outlands. I'm so frustrated, I could cry. But what do I do? Make him leave? My heart aches at the thought. He's clearly suffering, and it probably has nothing to do with real life and everything to do with him not taking his meds.

There's only one thing I can think to do. I put my hands on my hips and stand so close to him, he has no choice but to look me in the eyes. I keep my voice low but firm. "Darren, what you are saying is putting both of us in danger and I won't have it. I care about you, but I can't entertain this for a minute longer. It's ridiculous."

A look of deep hurt sinks his features. "It isn't ridiculous."

"Isn't it though? You, coming to my room hours after curfew, trying to get me to run away with you. To the *outlands*. At midnight. Are you trying to get me killed? I only just started taking care of myself."

He furrows his brow as if he's considering my words, but his eyes still hold a wild quality.

"I don't know what's going on with you," I say, "but I can tell you aren't yourself."

"How do you know? What if this is the real me?"

I pause, temporarily caught speechless. "If this is the real you, fine. But I can't stick around with you putting both our lives in danger. Weren't you the one who told me I deserved happiness? Well, this conversation isn't making me happy. It's *scaring* me."

He blinks a few times, then his face breaks, twisting as he covers it in his hands. "I'm sorry."

I put my hands on his heaving shoulders. "It's okay. You need to take your medication now."

"But—"

"No buts. I'm taking mine. You take yours." I retrieve the four pills I left on my desk. He watches me as I swallow them. "Now you."

He looks dejected as he swings his backpack from his shoulder, then digs inside. I hand him the water.

We stand in silence. I watch Darren swallow two large pills, wondering how quickly they will kick in. He's trembling. After a few tense minutes, he speaks. "I really am sorry. I'm an idiot. I don't know what came over me."

"Are you feeling better?"

He shakes his head. "No, but I will. I feel dizzy."

I take his hand and lead him to my bed, then pull his arms out of his jacket. "Lie down."

He doesn't argue, just kicks off his shoes and settles onto my mattress, eyes closed. I cover him with my blanket, and he scoots against the far wall. There's just enough room for me to crawl in next to him.

I know I should feel anxious about lying in bed with him, but I don't. I just feel tired. And confused.

Darren's breathing becomes slow and heavy. I watch him in the dark. Before tonight he'd been so strong, happy, and gentle. Tonight he was someone else. Terrified. Reckless. Angry.

I can't help but wonder. Which one is the real him?

CHAPTER FIFTEEN

I wake up to a kiss on my cheek and blink into the morning light. Darren's arm is around me, and he's looking at me with a mixture of confusion and tenderness.

"Hey," he says.

I turn toward him, feeling a blush creep up my cheeks. "How do you feel?"

He smiles. "So much better. Thanks for taking care of me last night."

"Of course," I say, then hesitate. "What was that all about anyway?"

"I don't know," he says with a shrug. "I hardly remember any of it."

"Did something happen yesterday? Something that made you want to stop taking your pills?"

He averts his gaze. Another shrug. "I think I just forgot to take them in the morning."

I narrow my eyes, wondering if he's telling the truth. "But you're feeling totally fine now?"

"Yeah. I'm really sorry you had to see me like that."

"It's okay." I put my hand on his arm. "Is that...how you normally are when you aren't being medicated?"

He meets my eyes with a laugh. "You mean crazy? God, I hope not."

"So that was just a one-time thing?"

He leans in close to me, brings his hand to the side of my face. "I promise you, Claire. You will never see me like that

again. Everything inside me wants to protect you, not scare
you. You know that, right?"

Our proximity stirs something inside me. My heart races as
I'm struck by the realization that Darren is in my bed. My *bed*.
And he's staring down at me like he realizes it too. I reach for
him, placing my hand behind his neck and pull him close until
our lips meet. This kiss isn't fierce like our others. There's passion, but there's an unprecedented gentleness too, like each kiss
is an apology from him and acceptance from me.

But that doesn't mean our kiss is entirely chaste, either.

Darren's hand leaves my face, trailing down my neck, trac-
ing my collarbone. Then his palm smooths over my shoulders,
down my arms, then stops at my hips where he gives me a
squeeze. He then runs his fingers along the waistband of my
jeans. It seemed sensible last night to sleep with my clothes on,
considering I had a delusional man in my bed. But now, I wish
I'd thrown caution to the wind.

My hands do their own exploring, moving down his chest,
around his waist, then under his shirt and up his smooth, firm
back. I feel his muscles flex with every movement he makes,
and I can feel myself arching toward him, my body begging to
be closer. His hand begins to creep from my waist up my stomach. My breaths are getting heavier. Our kisses deeper.

And then the moment shatters.

A persistent musical tone creeps upon my awareness, coming from somewhere in the middle of my room.

Darren lets out a frustrated groan, his hand over my
ribcage, then sits up.

My body shudders with disappointment. I was burning with curiosity to see where his hand would go next. Why couldn't we have had just a few minutes longer?

Darren makes his way slowly from my bed, then crouches over his discarded jacket that I'd removed from him last night. He reaches in the pocket and pulls out his reader. "My wakeup alarm," he says with a sigh. "I have to get ready for work."

My lips pull into a frown.

When his gaze returns to me, his face illuminates with a smile. "I really liked waking up next to you."

I return the grin. "So did I."

"Do you think you'd let me do it again?"

My stomach does a flip. Hell yes. "I suppose."

"Tonight? After work? Today's your day off, right?"

"Yes, yes, and yes," I say, trying to keep my voice cool and casual.

He puts on his jacket, shoulders his backpack, then comes to me for a kiss.

When he pulls away, I say, "Take your meds."

His lips pull into a crooked grin, then he reaches into his backpack for the pill bottle. After shaking a tablet into his hand, he downs the pill with a swig of water. "Done. See you tonight."

• • • •

WAITING FOR HIM TO return is agony. Since I'm off all day, I have nothing like work to distract me. I go out for groceries. Tidy my few possessions in my room. Wash my laundry in the communal laundry facility. Refold all my clothes.

As I'm getting dressed in my freshly washed jeans and favorite gray t-shirt, I pause, looking down at myself. It never occurred to me to care about how old my jeans are, how threadbare my shirt is or the way it slides off my shoulder a bit. At least my jeans hug my legs well, despite my lack of curves. I put my hands on my hips, wondering what they felt like when Darren put his hand there. Did he like what he found? Or am I too bony?

I move in front of my desk and stare in the mirror, surprised to see how much color has returned to my cheeks after weeks—months even—of looking so hollow and gaunt. The circles beneath my eyes have lessened, and there's less redness lingering in the whites of my eyes. I shake my hair from its messy bun and run my hands through it until my blond tresses fall in a wavy mass to my shoulders.

There was a time when I used to grow my hair nearly down to my waist and would have my mom curl it before school. My clothes were modern and new. That was back when I was allowed to care. Now that I'm a probationary, appearance is considered frivolous. Our clothing stores in the Public District consist of donations from Selects and older fashions that never sold well in Select stores. There is no beauty section at the Public market. No curling irons or hair ribbons. All I have in terms of makeup are a few leftover palettes and pencils from over two years ago.

I watch my frown reflected in the mirror and remember the bitterness in Darren's words last night. With a shake of my head, I turn away and look for other things to busy myself with.

• • • •

DARREN'S KNOCK COMES an hour before curfew. I hold my breath as I open the door, wondering which version of him I'll find.

He smiles and holds up a bag. "Illicit rooftop dinner? I brought food again."

I steal a kiss before I say, "Did you bring more wine too?" I'm only half-joking.

"Of course I did."

We make our way up the thirty flights of stairs to the roof. Again, Darren spreads out a ratty blanket and organizes our food. This time it's a hearty beef stew covered in a layer of flaky pastry, along with roasted broccoli and two rolls of bread. The wine is pale green. Just as gross in flavor as the last, but enjoyable all the same.

We keep drinking well after dinner is gone. Darren is staring into the distance, at the lights of Select city illuminating a portion of the sky. To the right of it, lies a smaller brightness, one of a different quality. More of a shimmering, sparkling. The Elite city. Where the Select city is bright and demanding of attention, the Elite is a sophisticated glow that gains attention from the sinuous curves of its impossibly high towers and gorgeous displays of iridescent light.

Darren points ahead at the Select District. "You can almost see them if you look hard enough."

I eye the tops of the buildings, wondering what he's seeing that I'm not. "What is it?"

"Mountains."

I'm confused until I realize he isn't referring to the city. He's referring to what's far behind it. Vague silhouettes of a landscape that rises and falls. No one looks to the outlands—not even the mountains—with any kind of reverence. We look at them like they're monsters, lying in wait with their toxic claws, eager to swallow us whole.

Seattle is a haven. Protection. One of the few lucky places untouched by war. There's only one city left in each territory that used to be considered a state. Our forefathers gathered us from across each state to settle into these cities as strength in numbers was our only chance for survival. I've heard rumors that some territories don't even have a city anymore, without a big enough population like ours to sustain it. Then again, we don't travel from city to city, nor do we hear much about the other cities at all. As far as I know, a rumor is just a rumor. Who knows what's really out there?

It's not for me to think about. It's not for *any* of us to think about.

The wistful expression on Darren's face as he stares at the hulking silhouettes makes my stomach sink with dread. "Did you mean any of what you said last night?"

He turns toward me, eyes locking with mine. "Yes." It comes out as a whisper.

I can hardly breathe. I want to look away from him, but I can't.

He leans closer, then laces his fingers through mine. "But that wasn't me. I'm not reckless like that. Sure, I believe some of those things. I'll bet most of us probationaries secretly do. But I'm not trying to run away or put you in danger."

I sigh. I'm disappointed, knowing my boyfriend—is that what he is?—has treasonous thoughts, but at least he's being honest.

"I could never want to leave," he says. "Not now. Not ever. Not when I have you."

My lips pull into a small smile. "Okay. I can accept that."

He leans closer, places a finger beneath my chin, then strokes his thumb along my jawline. "You make this world bearable. No—beautiful. You are like a bright light in a dark world, brighter than any light in the Elite city. Brighter than the stars. The moon."

His words are making me lightheaded, and I feel like my chest will explode. No one has ever talked to me like this before.

"Claire."

"Yeah?"

His hand pauses near my ear. "I love you."

The words send me reeling, making my throat feel tight and my heart feel like it's left my body completely to float in the sky above me. There's only one thing to say. "I love you too."

We come together with a kiss as tender as our kisses earlier this morning, and the eagerness I felt with him returns in full force. I'm so overcome with it, I can hardly remain upright, so I lean back on the blanket and pull him down with me. There, our hands pick up where they left off before his alarm brutally separated us. Mine rove his back, his chest. His slide up my waist, beneath my shirt, and over my stomach. I gasp and they rise higher, and I arch my back as I pull him against me.

Clothes. I have a sudden disdain for clothes, for anything that keeps us apart. With trembling fingers, I lift the hem of his shirt. He aids me by pulling it over his head, then slowly lifts me out of mine. Pants come off next. Then everything else.

We return to each other, vulnerable and naked beneath the night sky. He lifts himself on his forearms as his eyes take me in. I do the same, letting my hands move where my eyes go. He closes his eyes at my touch. When he opens them, they are full of hunger.

I smirk, delighted I have such power over him. But his power over me is equal. My body is quivering with my need for him, breaths ragged. I slide my hands to his lower back. Then I pull him down to me.

CHAPTER SIXTEEN

My body feels spent as we lay on the rooftop, feeling his kisses on the back of my neck. I shiver.

"Are you cold?" Darren whispers in my ear.

The shiver was more from delight, but as he says it, I realize I am getting cold. Probably due to my lack of clothes. "Maybe we should head back inside."

He kisses my cheek. "Come on."

We dress and Darren repacks his backpack. I feel like my legs are made of water as we make our way down the staircase and back to my room. Once inside, I go to the desk and take my pills. Darren does the same with his. After that, I strip back out of my jeans and sink into my bed. Darren follows, taking his place against the wall, arm pulling me close. I rest my head on his shoulder, my leg draping over his.

I feel his lips move to my ear. "Was that your first time?"

"Yes." I pull away, seeking his face in the dark. "Was it yours?"

His expression falls, and for a moment I feel a squeeze of disappointment. But I knew it was a possibility. He is two years older than me, after all. Not to mention that disarming smile of his. "No," he finally admits. "But I've never felt like that before. You're the first girl I've loved."

This, I'm surprised by. "Really?"

He nods. "What about you?"

I don't hesitate. "You are by far my first love."

He kisses me, and I feel his lips smiling against mine. "This has been the best night of my life."

I'm already replaying it in my head, and it isn't even over yet. "Mine too."

· · · ·

I REACH FOR HIM WHEN I wake, but all I find is empty mattress and cold sheets. With a rub of my eyes, I sit and look around my room. Maybe he got up before me to use my building's shower. But no, his things are all gone. Maybe he left for home to get ready for work but didn't want to wake me.

I stand and move to my desk, then pick up my reader. I press the screen, but it remains blank. "Damn," I say, realizing the battery is dead. When did I last charge it? I retrieve its charging disk from my backpack, then attach it to my reader. Nothing. I press the button on the bottom of the reader, trying to see if it will reset. My foot taps incessantly as I wait for it to turn back on.

"Finally." I let out an irritated grumble as the screen illuminates. No alerts pop up, so I tap the message icon. My heart drops, finding it empty. Not only have I not received any new messages, but all my previous ones, most of them from Darren, are missing as well. I click the contacts icon. Empty. My shoulders slump. When I reset my reader, it must have reset everything. I go to the files icon, expecting it to be empty too. But everything is there from the day I left my probation officer.

Okay, so maybe it only deleted everything since then.

I'm so anxious that I can't message Darren, but I remind myself that he's sure to message me at some point today. We work the same hours, so as long as he doesn't have to stay late, there's a good chance I'll see him on the way to or from work.

But I don't see him. Not on the bus, not on the rail. No messages come from him no matter how many times I sneak a look at my reader during my laundry shift. He isn't on the rail platform, or anywhere I look on my way home that night.

I'm trying not to panic, trying not to go to the worst-case scenario, but it's impossible not to. After all the attention he gave me earlier this week, I can't help but feel like something is wrong.

What if he regrets what we did last night?

I shake the thought from my head. He told me last night was the best night of his life. He didn't have to say that.

I get to my apartment building, and my last hope dies in my chest when I find him neither in the courtyard nor waiting outside my door. My stomach is a roiling mess as I look around my room, trying to remember the moment he removed his arm from over my body. When did he leave? I can't even recall when my head no longer rested on his chest. He was there when I fell asleep. Gone when I woke. What happened in between?

My eyes flick to the bottles of pills on my desk, and I glare at them. Maybe he tried to wake me this morning, but I was too deeply asleep. I check my reader. Still no messages from him.

What if he messaged me when my reader was dead? What if he said something sweet, but thinks I never responded on purpose? What if he thinks I'm avoiding *him*?

I feel like I'm losing my mind.

"Damn it, Darren," I say to my reader. "Where are you?"

• • • •

I DON'T SLEEP THAT night. I don't take my pills. Until I know where Darren is, I blame my medication for making me miss his exit from my room. Besides, I keep hoping I'll hear a knock at my door at any moment. But it doesn't come that night or the next morning. It's Saturday, and our work shifts line up again. He has to be at the bus stop. Or the rail.

He isn't.

I can barely focus in the laundry room. Marlene and the other women try to engage me in conversation, but I can't keep up with what they're talking about, much less chime in. I'm torn between anger and worry and fear. What if something happened to him?

I think back to that night he came to my room acting crazy. He said he felt like someone was following him. Was that part true? *Was* someone following him?

I'm biting my nails, fingertips raw and tender, all the way home on the rail. I watch out the window of the bus, seeking any sign of Darren. When I reach our housing center, I circle building four, where Darren lives. I want to kick myself for never asking which room he's in. How has he seen my room, yet I've never seen his?

It's almost curfew, but I'm still rounding his building, over and over. I see a shadowed figure enter the courtyard, and my heart races. But it can't be him. Too short. Too round. I approach the man anyway. He startles when he sees me racing toward him.

"Hey," I say. "Do you know Darren—" Panic rises in my throat as I realize another fact missing from my mind. How have I never asked his last name? Have I told him mine?

"Darren," the man echoes.

"Yeah. Tall, dark curly hair. Dark green jacket. A couple years older than me."

He shrugs. "That could be a lot of people."

I clench my hands into fists and grind my teeth to keep from shouting in frustration. The man turns away, but I persist. "You don't know anyone named Darren who lives here?"

He glares, his patience wearing thin. "No. Now get wherever you belong before curfew."

I let out a groan, then stomp away from the building toward mine. Up the stairs, I take two at a time, then pass my floor and keep going up, up, up. I'm out of breath as I reach the roof, but I don't care. I turn in a circle once I reach the center of the roof, but there's nothing. No sign of him. No forgotten reader, no shred of clothing. Nothing to suggest we were ever there two nights ago, naked in each other's arms. My knees go weak at the thought.

I return to my room, biting my nails again, even though there's nothing left to bite. Once inside I check my reader, but just like every other time, there's nothing to see.

I can no longer ride the hope that Darren's schedule got crazy and I'm overreacting. It's been a full two days, and Darren hasn't contacted me once. There are only two possibilities. Either he's avoiding me on purpose. Or something very, very bad has happened to him.

CHAPTER SEVENTEEN

I leave my apartment before sunrise and stand outside building four. Darren is off Sundays, so I can't rely on him following any kind of schedule. Still, I wait. If I stand outside his building long enough, I'm bound to see him.

Right?

It's almost noon—I know this because I'm constantly checking my reader—when I see an enforcer round the corner of the building into the courtyard. I've been standing in the courtyard since I got here, moving from one side to the other, questioning everyone I can. Everyone so far has responded to me the way the man did last night. They don't know Darren. Too impatient to care. Could someone have reported me to the enforcers?

I'm about to turn tail and run when another thought crosses my mind. Enforcers may be terrifying with their black helmets, their padded suits, and their thick clubs, but they are supposed to protect us. Or our city, at least.

It's a long shot, but I head toward him, heart racing as I close the distance.

"Badge," he demands before I can stop in front of him.

I reach into the pocket of my jacket. My fingers are quivering as I fumble to separate my city badge from my room key. When I hand it to him, he scans it. After a few seconds, the light turns green. He's about to hand it back to me when he pauses, looks back at the panel on his wrist.

"Why aren't you in the Select District right now?" His voice is brusque as he eyes me through the visor of his helmet.

I'm caught off guard. The Select District? Why would I be there? "I don't work today."

"That's not what this says. Says you work in the city Sundays. Extended curfew clearance, too."

My mouth falls open as I search for words. Dr. Shelia must not have filed for my city clearance to change when she arranged my resignation from my jobs. I raise my hand, showing him the remnants of the stitches that haven't dissolved yet. "I'm injured. I don't work today." At least both things are true.

He stares at me a few seconds longer, then hands me my badge. "I've gotten reports of a non-resident loitering and harassing the tenants of building four. Is that you?"

I nod, though it terrifies me to do so. "I'm sorry. I should have come to the precinct sooner instead of trying to handle this myself. I've been looking for a...friend who lives here. Something's wrong. I haven't seen him in days, which is highly unusual."

"Friend's name?"

"Well, here's the thing...I only know his first name. It's Darren. He lives in the building, but I'm not sure which room."

I can see his eyes narrow through his visor. "You are looking for a friend whose name and room number you don't know."

"Correct." Can he see how badly I'm trembling?

"It doesn't sound like you're very good friends."

"We are, it's just—"

"When did you last see him?"

"Thursday night," I say.

"So it's been less than seventy-two hours."

My throat feels dry. "Yes."

"There's nothing I can do about that. If you haven't seen this friend of yours in three days, it's probably for a good reason."

Tears glaze my eyes. "But I'm really worried about him."

What I can see of his expression softens. "Look, kid, Publics can't report other non-kin citizens until a week has passed, and without a last name, you can't report him missing at all."

My shoulders fall and hot tears stream down my cheeks. "What if something bad happened?"

The enforcer shifts awkwardly from foot to foot. Finally, he says, "If he's actually missing, his employers would already have reported him to the precinct. We'd already be on it."

I want to feel comfort at that, knowing his absence would surely be noted where he works, if he's truly absent at all. But what would enforcers even do, aside from clear out his apartment so they can rent it out to someone else, then file an arrest warrant for missing work? It's not like they'd go looking for him or treat it like an actual missing person's case. Publics don't matter like that. Probationaries even less.

"You can't loiter here, regardless of what you think has happened to your friend." His harsh tone has returned. "Get back to your own building."

I nod and turn away, my vision swimming through tears. When I'm in front of building seven, I look behind me. The enforcer didn't follow. Good. Instead of turning into the courtyard of my apartment, I head to the bus stop. I have other plans.

• • • •

I ARRIVE AT THE CITY and immediately seek out the Golden Tempest where Darren said his friend works. Since it belongs to the Hightower Hotel, it isn't far from where I work. All hotels are within a six-block radius of each other. It's mostly Elites who work in the Select city who stay at these hotels. I'm surprised there are so many. Why would an Elite choose to stay anywhere but their own shining city?

I find the Hightower Hotel, then the Golden Tempest, which has its own entrance. But I don't go inside. This is where my plan brought me, but I didn't think of what to do next. I can't just go up to the host's desk and ask to see a man named Mitchell, a man I've never met and know nothing about, aside from the fact that he provides Darren with illicit table scraps and leftovers.

I hover in front of the door, watching patrons come in and out. Then I round the building to the alley, where I find dumpsters and back doors. This is where I wait. Almost an hour passes before one of the doors opens and a man in a black uniform—not much different from the ones I wore at my restaurant jobs—comes out with a black plastic bag. The uniform is promising. It means he isn't a supervisor.

I approach him as he tosses the bag into the dumpster. "Do you know Mitchell? Who works here?"

The man startles, then narrows his eyes with suspicion.

"Please, it's important."

He puts his hands on his hips as he assesses me. "Yeah. I know him."

Relief washes over me. "Is he here today?"

"Maybe."

"Can you tell him to come out here when he gets a break? I'll wait until he's off if I must, but it's really important that I speak to him. It's about a mutual friend who I think is in trouble."

The man's expression softens, and he nods. "I'll tell him."

When he goes back inside, I start pacing and biting my nails. Every time the door opens, I stop and watch expectantly, hoping the person who comes out will be looking for me. Hours pass and the only people I see are bearing garbage bags; not one gives pause, much less scans the alley as if they are expecting someone.

It's nearing 6 p.m. before a new face arrives. He looks a few years older than me, and when he enters the alley, he seems hesitant, eyes scanning left and right before they fall on me waiting behind a stack of empty crates. We lock eyes and he shuts the door behind him.

"I hear you're looking for me," he says, brow furrowed. His eyes are a pale blue, his head shaved, and a shadow of stubble covers his chin. He'd be handsome if I didn't compare him to Darren.

My mouth feels dry as I find my voice. "You're Mitchell?"

He nods.

"Do you know Darren?"

He stares at me, but I can't tell if it's from suspicion or confusion. "Who?"

"Darren."

He shakes his head. "Don't know a Darren."

My heart sinks. Then again, maybe he thinks I'm here to confront him about providing Darren contraband. "Darren told me about you. He said you're his friend. I think he's in trouble, or something bad has happened. I just want to know. Have you seen him the last two days?"

"I told you, I don't know who you're talking about. I don't know a Darren." His voice is even. But is he lying? He has to be! Darren knew about *him*, at least enough to tell me where he works. So there's a connection somewhere. Is it possible Darren goes by another name?

"He's the one you give leftover food to. You should have seen him on Thursday night. He got food for us. Stew, broccoli, bread rolls, wine—"

"I told you, I don't know him. And I didn't give anyone food on Thursday."

"I'm not here to get him or you into trouble. I'm here because—"

"I. Don't. Know. Him." His face is flushed. "Now get out of here before I call an enforcer."

Before I can say a word more, he opens the door and slams it behind him. I stare at it for countless minutes, hoping it will open again, hoping he'll reappear and apologize. Hoping he'll tell me about Darren.

It doesn't happen.

When I realize this, tears well in my eyes and I slam my back into the wall of the building to keep myself from collapsing. What the hell is happening? Nothing makes sense! Darren is nowhere to be found. He hasn't contacted me. The person he's supposed to know claims not to know him. What do I do now? I already know enforcers won't help. Perhaps if I were an Elite or even a Select...

I stand up straight, an idea coming to mind. It's a long shot, but it might be my last hope.

CHAPTER EIGHTEEN

I don't stop until I reach the frosted glass door to Dr. Shelia's clinic. Only then do I hesitate, considering whether this is a good idea. She did call herself my advocate. If anyone were to help me, it would be her. I open the door and try my best to summon both calm and confidence as I march into the waiting room.

Emily looks surprised to see me. "Oh, hi, Claire. You don't have an appointment today, do you?"

I squeeze my fingertips into my palms to keep my hands from shaking. "No, but I was hoping she might have a minute to spare for me today. I can wait however long it takes."

"Dr. Shelia doesn't normally work Sundays."

It hadn't even occurred to me that she might not be in. "Is she not here, then? Why are you here?"

"Dr. Shelia came in for an emergency call with a patient, so I was called in to work too. I can check in with her after she gets out of her appointment and see if she can see you after. Does that work?"

I nod.

"What should I tell her your visit is regarding?"

I open my mouth, but I'm not sure what to say. The truth? "I'm worried about something that's happened, and I'm not sure who else to go to."

Emily can't keep the concern out of her eyes, but she plasters a fake smile over her lips. "I'll let her know. Have a seat."

I sit, though I can hardly hold still. My legs shake whether I cross my ankles or force my feet firmly into the ground. My hands won't stop moving, so I alternate between biting my nails and tapping my fingers on the armrest. Time seems to tick by at a snail's pace.

Finally, a man emerges from the back hall and enters the waiting room. His shoulders droop, footsteps shuffling as he checks in with Emily. When he turns away from the desk and brushes past me toward the door, I catch a glimpse of his face. It's flushed, his eyes bloodshot, a look of terror in them. I sit upright, chilled, as I watch him close the door behind him.

"Dr. Shelia will speak to you now," Emily says, stealing my attention back to her. "Go on back. She's already there."

The man is forgotten as I stand, my anxiety building higher with every step I take toward her office. There's no guarantee Dr. Shelia can help me, or that she'll even respond well to this impromptu meeting.

I enter the room and find Dr. Shelia already at her desk, smiling. She looks uncharacteristically happy, especially considering the state of her patient who just left. "Come in, Claire. Have a seat."

I take my usual seat on the couch but can't bring myself to meet her eyes. I know if I do, I'll see her smile falter. It will be replaced with judgment. Worry. Disappointment. She'll know I'm a wreck. She'll know I've stopped taking my medication.

It doesn't take her long to catch on. "Maybe you should lie down," she says.

I breathe a sigh of gratitude and lay back on the couch. My heart is racing so fast, I feel like the couch will shake from the force of it.

"I'm glad you came to me, Claire. Emily said you're worried about something and needed someone to talk to. Tell me what's going on." Her voice is smooth, calm, even. It helps put some of my nerves at ease.

I take a deep breath and let it out slowly. "Darren is missing. He has been since Friday morning. I haven't heard from him. I haven't seen him. Something has to be wrong, but no one has been able to help me."

"You've tried contacting him?"

"That's the worst part! I woke up Friday morning and found my reader had died overnight. The only way to get it to turn on was to reset it. Once I got it working again, his contact code and all our previous messages were gone."

"I imagine that must be frustrating for you. Still, it's been less than three days. Why do you think something is wrong? He could be busy with work or other things."

I shake my head. "Our relationship isn't like that. He's tried to see me every day since we began seeing each other. And if we haven't had time to hang out, he always messages."

"Relationship dynamics can shift. You've only been together a couple weeks. Perhaps his need to communicate every day has cooled off."

"No, he wouldn't do that. Not after..."

"Not after what?" There's a knowing quality to her tone.

I feel a blush creeping up my cheeks. Did I think I could show up here unannounced and not have to talk about what happened between me and Darren? I decide to start with something I don't feel embarrassed to confess. "He said he loved me, and I said it back."

I can feel her eyes on me, but she doesn't say anything in response.

The heat is still rising in my face. I can't stand her silence, so I say, "I know he meant it. We both did. He wouldn't stop speaking to me out of nowhere."

"What else happened?"

Damn it all, she knows. I suppose that's what it takes to do her job well. My fingers are curling and uncurling, so I bind them together, then wring my hands. "We slept together."

Silence again.

"He said it was the best night of his life, and I know he meant it. When I woke up, he was gone. I don't even remember him leaving."

Dr. Shelia shifts in her chair. "You know, it isn't uncommon for young men to fear intimacy. It may have felt right in the moment, but maybe afterward he realized he needed some time to come to terms with his feelings about your relationship. If that's the case, there is likely nothing to worry about. He'll come around when he's had a chance to think things through. If your relationship means as much to him as it does to you, this won't keep him away for long."

"But I know him," I argue. "He would never ignore me like this after something so important."

"Do you really know him, Claire?"

I stiffen. My stomach sinks as I try to find a compelling argument to prove I do, in fact, know him, but all evidence points to the contrary. I know what building he lives in, but not the room. I know what type of work he does, but not where. I never even learned his last name.

I try to think through everything I've told him about myself. Did I leave out any of these facts? Were we both so wrapped up in spending time together that we never bothered to learn any minute details? Or did he purposefully withhold them from me?

I shudder at the thought. No, he wouldn't have done it on purpose. What we had was real. It was more real than anything I've experienced in my life. "I may not know everything about him, but I know enough to be sure he wouldn't act this way. Besides, I know his schedule, and I haven't seen him at the bus stop, on the rail, outside his building. Nowhere."

"You've been waiting outside his building?"

I swallow hard, then nod. "I waited all morning today until an enforcer came. I tried to get him to help me, but he didn't take my worries seriously. Without his last name or any connection of kinship, I can't report him as missing."

"And you shouldn't," she says. "You don't know that he is missing. Besides, if he is, his employers will be the first to report him."

"That's what the enforcer said." A thought comes to mind, sending a ripple of energy through me. I sit up, eyes locking on Dr. Shelia. "Is that something someone like you would have access to? Some kind of database for missing people being reported?"

She watches me, eyes narrowed. I feel cold beneath her scrutiny, but I can't look away. I'm too full of hope that she'll say yes. She leans forward in her chair. "Lay back down, Claire. I think we should first discuss why you were outside Darren's building all morning."

"I told you. I know something is wrong. He has to be in trouble."

"Then why were you looking for him? If you know something is wrong and you think he's missing, then why did you expect to find him at home?"

I consider her words, agitation making my shoulders tense. "I wanted to prove to myself that he *is* missing."

"Why? Because you're afraid of the alternative? That he's avoiding you?"

I stammer, before saying, "Well, of course I'm worried about that possibility, but I know that's not the case."

"Go ahead and lie back down."

I grind my teeth, then do as told.

"Have you been taking your medication?"

"No. I stopped after I found Darren missing."

"Why?"

"I'm too anxious to sleep."

"If you took your medication, you'd sleep just fine. You know this."

The agitation within me is spreading like a fire. I can feel it crawling up my spine, down to my fingertips. She doesn't understand. I *can't* sleep.

"Why are you afraid of sleep?"

I frown and turn to face her. "Afraid? What are you talking about?"

"You're afraid to sleep. Tell me why."

"Because...Darren went missing while I was sleeping. I don't want to sleep in case that's when I finally hear from him. I want to be there for him when he needs me."

"Why else?"

"There is no other reason. And it's not fear, it's me being cautious."

"You were afraid to sleep before you met Darren. I thought it was general trauma, but I don't think that's the entire story. Why are you afraid to sleep?"

I look away from her, tears welling in my eyes. I squeeze my eyes shut, fighting the tightening in my chest.

Dr. Shelia's voice comes softly. "You can tell me, Claire. I'm here for you."

It comes out with a sob. "My mom died while I was sleeping." The memory seizes me—finding my mother lifeless in her bed, without warning. Without a goodbye. All I got from her were her last words. *Rise up, my sweet one. You are worth more than this.* She'd roused me from sleep in the middle of the night with them, along with a soft kiss. I felt the kiss on my cheek, heard the words, but I didn't wake enough to respond. I just floated back to sleep, no idea that those words would be her last.

Dr. Shelia doesn't speak; she just lets me cry. When I begin gasping for air, she fetches me a cup of water from the waiting room, then opens the window in her office. This helps me catch my breath as the tears continue to pour freely.

My tears are long past spent by the time Dr. Shelia speaks again. Her words come softly to me. "You're planting the weight of your mother's death into Darren's perceived disappearance. You are associating both acts with the trauma of being abandoned. What is happening with Darren is triggering these memories inside you. If you detach this trauma from the situation, you'll see what's happening with Darren is entirely normal."

I want to argue. Darren's disappearance didn't trigger any thoughts of my mom's death, but could she be right? Could there be some underlying association making me perceive my current events beneath the clouds of my past?

It's possible, and I'd almost prefer for her to be right. If Darren is simply avoiding me due to some fear of intimacy, that means he could come back. He could show up at my apartment tonight, apology in hand. We could pick up where we left off.

Then another memory comes to mind—Darren, eyes wild, talking about how he's being followed. I open my mouth to tell Dr. Shelia about this, then snap it closed again. What good could it do? She already thinks I'm overreacting. I close my eyes and try to let Dr. Shelia's theory bring me peace. My racing heart begins to slow, and my muscles begin to unclench.

"I really am glad you came to me," Dr. Shelia says. "You are welcome to come to me at any time. I will make time for you. And message me if you have any unsettling thoughts. For now, I want you to go home and put Darren out of your mind. Spend some time doing what Darren is likely doing. Think about what your relationship with him means to you. Think about what you need from him going forward. A last name is a good start."

There's humor in her voice, but I don't feel like laughing. Still, I force a smile and say my thanks. I leave her office, leave the city, head back to the Public District. I feel empty. Raw.

No matter how much I try, no matter how much Dr. Shelia might be right, there's no way I can put Darren out of my mind.

CHAPTER NINETEEN

The next few days go by in a blur. It's like the days following my mom's death all over again. The numbness has returned. I hate that I feel this way, that I'm letting some guy—or lack of—determine my mental state. But it isn't just depression over him disappearing. There's still the fear that my original theory is correct.

That somewhere out there, Darren is in trouble.

But I can't think about that, because thinking about it makes me fall apart. And I can't fall apart because there's work to be done. Laundry to wash.

Cue the numbness.

It's better not to feel anything than to feel like my world is falling away beneath me.

The women in the laundry room have gone back to not speaking to me. They tried to get me involved in their conversations, but I can only manage a grunt here and there at best these days. Wednesday comes around, and I have another appointment with Dr. Shelia. It's more of the same. Talking about my mom. Talking about my abandonment issues. Talking about how I should be taking my pills and getting sleep.

She shows me a mirror to make her point. I stare at my reflection, but all I can do is convulse with a single laugh that doesn't make it out of my mouth. The radiance I saw looking back at me before I spent my last night with Darren is gone. Was it ever there to begin with? The circles have returned to their place beneath my eyes, darker than ever. My skin is so pale, I swear it's translucent. And my eyes. The blue looks nothing like the summer sky, like my mom used to compare them to. It looks more like the shade of a corpse. I look away with a sigh, and Dr. Shelia watches me, face full of concern. When Dr. Grand comes in, she tells me how my vitals are slipping, but I hardly hear her words.

I leave in a daze, barely registering my travels down the streets of the city, past the flashing advertisements on every corner, past the restaurants, windows, people. I don't remember getting on the rail or the bus. I'm not sure where my thoughts are as I walk home because I'm not paying attention to those either. Thoughts are dangerous. They revolve around Darren.

I know it must be nearing curfew by the time the housing centers are in view because the streets around me have grown quiet. That strikes me as odd, considering I'm not out past extended curfew tonight. Just regular curfew. This clears my head a little, bringing my thinking mind out from hiding.

As I walk down the street leading to my apartment, I quicken my pace. There's still a hint of light in the sky, but that doesn't mean I like walking past alleyways at night. My eyes are fixed firmly ahead when I hear a sound to my right coming from the alley. I give it a wide berth and am about to hurry past when motion catches my eye. I freeze, startling further away from it. That's when a figure rises, shadowed beneath the growing darkness between the two tall buildings, halfway down the alley. When he's on his feet, I only need to see a hint of his face to recognize him.

"Darren?"

He's filthy, clothes stained and torn, face bruised and bloody. "Claire." His voice comes out with a cry. "Oh my God, Claire. Are you really here?"

I'm frozen in horror, in confusion, until my feet remember how to move. We start toward each other at the same time, tears of relief already streaming down my face. It feels like an eternity stands between us, and we move like there isn't a moment to spare.

But it isn't fast enough.

A door in the alley opens between us, and Darren stumbles, nearly falling in his haste to press himself as far as he can from it. I hesitate, watching as an arm clears the door, followed by a body dressed in black. It isn't the black of an enforcer, but he's covered nearly as much, a knit hat over his head and a thick, black jacket zipped to his neck. I can't make out his face, but his intent is clear as he lunges for Darren. "There he is," the man grumbles, locking his fingers around Darren's wrist and hauling him toward the door.

"Darren!" I shout, torn between running toward him and running away.

The man's eyes find mine, and what I can see of them looks malicious. "There's a girl out here! Get her!"

The man pulls Darren behind the door as another shadowed figure emerges.

"Run!" calls Darren's voice, even though I can no longer see him.

My feet obey before my mind does, and I'm flying away from the alley, following the familiar path to my apartment building. While I've always been a fast walker, running has never been my strength, and the weight of my backpack is slowing me down. But I keep running, breaths heaving, throat constricting, ignoring the sound of the footsteps gaining on me.

As my courtyard comes into view, I sprint harder, relieved when I see several people making their way up the different staircases to their rooms.

"Help!" I shout, uncaring how badly I startle them. I run to the nearest person, a woman. She backs up, hand to her chest. When I reach her, I look behind me. I release a heavy breath, seeing I wasn't followed into the courtyard.

The woman puts a reluctant hand on my shoulder, and I return to face her. Three other people are beginning to gather. "What is it?" Her voice is more impatient than kind, but at least I have her attention.

"I'm being followed," I say through gasping breaths. "There was a man. In an alley. He took my friend. He's hurting him right now. They came after me because I saw."

The woman furrows her brow. "You should get to your room. Lie down for a bit."

I shake my head. "Lie down? When my friend is being tortured? No! We need to help him!"

Her eyes go wide and she takes a step higher on the staircase. "I'm not getting involved with anything like that."

Two of the other people are walking away from me too, but one stays. He's an older man, but I barely see him. All I can see is Darren's beaten face.

"If you want to call an enforcer, I will wait with you until one arrives," he says.

I sigh. I'm not sure what more I expected. It's not like I could bring a gang of apartment tenants to confront the men in the alley. No. An enforcer is my only hope.

By the time one arrives, my nerves are frayed, as if they weren't already. I'm surprised my heart hasn't ruptured from its speed. I meet the enforcer in the middle of the courtyard and open my mouth to explain.

"Badge," he says before I can utter a word.

I snap my mouth shut, then retrieve my badge.

He scans it. "You're out past curfew."

I stare at him, taken aback. "I called you for help."

"You shouldn't be out past curfew."

"I know, but someone's in trouble." I rush to tell my story before he can interrupt. I know I must sound crazy with how fast I'm talking, and the way he stares at me beneath his helmet after I've finished my story confirms his doubts.

"Let me get this straight," he finally says. "You were walking home and passed an alley where you saw your missing friend being taken by a strange man into one of the buildings."

"Yes."

"Maybe he lives there."

"He doesn't live there. Besides, why would someone drag him inside like that, all bloodied?"

He ignores me. "Maybe he works there."

That makes just as little sense as him living there. "He works in the Select District."

"What building was it?"

I hesitate, trying to remember what buildings belong to that particular alley. "I don't know," I say, then rush to add, "but I remember what alley. I can show you where I saw him."

He lets out an irritated sigh. "Fine."

I lead the way back toward the alley. "I was followed by one of the men up until I reached my courtyard." I look left and right, wondering if I'll spot someone lurking in the shadows, then look at the enforcer. He doesn't appear the least bit alarmed. He doesn't even have his club out. "Aren't you going to call for reinforcements?"

I imagine him rolling his eyes because his tone reflects it. "If what you say proves to be true, I'll call for others. Until then, I am only checking on what you think you saw."

"It could be dangerous. There were at least two of them."

He says nothing.

We reach the alley, my blood cold at the memory still fresh in my mind. I lead the enforcer to where I last saw Darren and stop in front of the door he'd been taken into. "Here. This is where they took him."

The enforcer looks the door up and down, shining a beam of light from the panel on his wrist, then points to a plaque in the middle of the door. "Laundromat," he says. "This one closed a year ago. There's nothing here now."

That doesn't surprise me. "That's where they're hiding him."

"Hiding him," he echoes.

I'm so frustrated with his lack of concern, I could scream. "Yes, where they are torturing him."

"Why?"

"I don't know, but shouldn't you go in there and rescue him? Please. He could be dead already."

He lets out a sigh that sounds more like a groan, then tries the handle. It doesn't budge. He stares at it for a moment, then looks back toward the street. "Come on, we'll try the front." His voice sounds less agitated now, but he doesn't sound worried in the least.

We make our way to the front of the building where the old laundromat is boarded up. He shines his lights between the bars covering the door, then between the slats of wood sealing the window. "Broken," he says, then begins prying a few boards at the bottom and side to reveal an opening. Once clear, he steps through, and I follow.

I'm holding my breath, trembling from head to toe as we walk through the abandoned laundromat. A few old machines remain, but it seems most have been hauled away, leaving light spaces on the walls where they used to be. Like mechanical ghosts.

Every sound we make sends my heart higher and higher in my throat. I expect the men to surge toward us at any moment. Why hasn't he called for reinforcements yet?

As we make our way further back, toward the rooms that were probably used for office or break rooms, my eyes search for any sign of Darren. Clothes. Footprints. Blood. I shudder. But aside from a few scraps of fabric, metal parts, and some shattered glass there's nothing. No one.

We approach the door to the back rooms, and I'm trembling from head to toe. If Darren isn't out here, he must be in there. The enforcer takes a slow step forward, then another. He puts his hand on the metal door, then moves it to the handle. Turns it. I clutch my chest as the door swings out, then blink a few times to fully register what I'm seeing. This is no back room, no office. This is the alley we just vacated.

"No!" I push past the enforcer into the alley, looking left and right. My shoulders sink, and my knees feel like they are going to collapse. "They took him already. They knew I'd bring an enforcer here." I turn toward the man. "We need to look again. There might be clues."

His hand wraps around my wrist, and I look down at it. Only, it's not his hand. It's a cuff, and he holds the other end.

"You're coming with me."

CHAPTER TWENTY

I've never been arrested before, but all I can think about is Darren. Not even the cost to my credits or the possible extension to my probationary sentence clears him from my mind.

I saw him tonight. He really is in trouble.

I was right all along.

But being right doesn't help when I'm stuck in a jail cell. I'm the only one in it, which I could be grateful for, but the amenities in a Public cell make my apartment feel Elite. There's nothing but a narrow bench affixed to the wall and a filthy toilet. No bed. No blankets. The cell is barred by a metal door with a thick glass window. My eyes are affixed on this window as I sit on the bench, waiting to hear what they will do with me next. I'm sure I'll have to spend the night. But after that?

I see movement through the window and I stand. As the door opens, I am shocked to see Dr. Shelia enter. An enforcer trails behind her, carrying an old folding chair. I'm too stunned to move or speak as the enforcer places the chair in the middle of the room then leaves, closing the door behind him.

She sits on the folding chair, then motions toward the bench behind me. "Have a seat."

Didn't we just do this a few hours ago? But I don't argue. I return to the bench and cross my arms over my chest. "What are you doing here?" My voice comes out toneless.

She eyes me with her cool stare. "It seems again I have to rescue you from your lack of self-care. Last time this happened, I thought we moved beyond it."

I lean forward. "My lack of self-care? Are you kidding me? I was right about Darren. I saw him tonight."

"Like when you saw your mother? On the same street, was it?"

I'm so shocked, all I can do is stare at her. "This isn't anything like when I saw my mom. He was actually there. He said my name, he told me to run."

"Your mother said your name."

"This was real, and I don't know how else to prove—" An idea comes to mind. I'd be giddy if the circumstances weren't so dire. "Watch my footage."

"Your footage?"

I nod. "As my psychiatrist, you must have access to my Reality footage."

"I don't."

"You're an Elite, aren't you?"

"Yes, but considering our professional relationship, I am not permitted to watch your Reality lifestream. It goes against the ethics of my job."

"I don't care about the ethics! Someone's life is in danger. If you watch, you'll know I was right. You can report the incident to the Elite enforcement. Someone would listen to you!"

"Not even an Elite has access to replay footage. Not unless your lifestream is picked up for a show."

My heart sinks. "There has to be a way. You could speak to my agent, Kori Wan. If she knew what was happening, she'd give you replay access."

"Do you want a show, Claire?"

I blink a few times to clear my mind. Why did she change the subject? "A show? No. That's the last thing I want."

"If you had a show that went viral, you'd be able to pay off your debts far faster than working. You'd be able to make your mother's last words a reality. You'd be able to rise faster than ever before."

I shrug. "So?"

"I could see the potential for all these mishaps to benefit your lifestream. There are few things more interesting than watching someone lose their mind on Reality viewing."

Heat rises to my face when I realize what she's insinuating. "You think I'm making all of this up on purpose."

"Are you making it up on accident?"

"I'm not making it up at all! I'm not making any of this up! A man I love is missing. He's being tortured. And no one believes me." I rise to my feet, turning my back toward her. "You know what? Maybe I do want a show. Because if a viral lifestream brings attention to the truth, the truth about Darren, then maybe someone will help him. Unlike you. You only pretend to help me, but all you want is for me to take your pills and become a graph of orderly rows making orderly progress, so you can feel like you're good at your job. Never mind the reality of the situation, so long as the numbers look how you want them to."

"I'm trying to help you." There's hurt in her tone, but it doesn't make me feel bad for what I said. "I have always been your advocate and continue to be now."

I whirl around and take a step toward her. "Then why are you trying to convince me I'm crazy? Why aren't you doing everything you can to help Darren? If you want to help me, that's what will."

Dr. Shelia's face falls, but she doesn't say anything. We eye each other for countless minutes, my chest heaving as I try not to consider the possible ramification for speaking to an Elite like I just did.

Footsteps sound outside the cell, and an enforcer's face appears in the window. He opens the door, breaking the tension. "Time's up. Either she goes with you or she stays overnight."

My eyes go wide. After what I said, there's no way she'll do anything but leave me here.

Dr. Shelia nods. "Sign her into my care. I'll take her to her apartment."

I'm almost too shocked to follow Dr. Shelia out of the cell. When I finally get my legs moving, I trail behind her to the front desk where she signs a few documents, then outside where a sleek black car awaits. It must be hers. You never see cars in the Public District.

A driver gets out and opens the door to the backseat where Dr. Shelia scoots in. "Come," she says to me. I can hardly contain my trembling as I take the seat next to her. Never before has Dr. Shelia's status come to my attention so strongly as it is now. She's an Elite. She has a car. And a driver. A *human* driver. Only the wealthiest Elites splurge on hiring human drivers, as automated driving systems are far more affordable. That's all that exists in the Select District.

Yet despite her status, she works in the Select District with people like me. She's come to my aid twice now outside of business hours. And I yelled at her.

Shame heats my cheeks as the car rolls into motion. "Will there be any repercussions?"

Dr. Shelia is looking out the window at the black streets. "No. I told them you are mentally unwell and are not responsible for certain actions in your current state. I have, however, promised them you are in recovery and are capable of being on your own without causing any more trouble for the precinct. I hope I'm right." She turns her head toward mine and fixes me with her glare.

I swallow hard. "I'm sorry for what I said back there. I didn't mean it. But I am being honest about what I saw. Darren was there."

"I know you believe that's the truth."

My chest feels tight and tears sting my eyes. She won't believe me. What's the use? I turn toward the window, staring at nothing until the car comes to a stop outside my building. I reach for the door but Dr. Shelia grabs my wrist.

"Everything I do is in your best interest. You know that right?"

I nod but don't meet her eyes.

"I want you to go inside, take your medication, and get some sleep. I promise you, if you do, you will feel so much better about everything."

I mutter my thanks as the driver opens my door. I hurry into the courtyard and up the stairs, passing my floor and racing all the way to the roof. There, I fall to my knees beneath the stars, the black sky, the crescent moon, and let it all out with silent tears. The tension between me and Dr. Shelia. The pain of seeing Darren again only to lose him seconds later. The humiliation of no one believing me.

As I stand, I feel empty again and begin to slip back into numb. I take a step toward the staircase but feel something beneath my shoe. Nearly tripping, I shuffle aside, revealing a plastic cylinder, broken in two. I reach for it and hold it up to the moonlight.

A wine cork.

I pocket it as if it's a piece of Darren. In a way, it is. It reminds me of the night we spent together, of the words he said to me. It reminds me what I'm fighting for, no matter who believes me.

I go to my room and throw my backpack on the floor, then take out my reader to give me some light. My eyes fall on the bottles of pills on my desk. I grimace at them, then sweep them into my wastebasket. I stare into the darkness of my room. And I come up with a plan.

CHAPTER TWENTY-ONE

The next day is my day off, but I head to the Select District. As far as I know, my city clearance remains in effect every day of the week. When I get off the rail, I head to the Salish. I take a deep breath then enter the back room, the locker room, then the kitchen. A dishwasher stands at the sink, but it isn't Molly. It's too early for her shift to start, and she's not who I came here to see, anyway.

I wait until Mr. Evans is finished delivering orders to the cooks before I approach him. He looks surprised when he sees me, then irritation flashes over his face. "Here to beg for your job back? You've already been replaced."

I try to keep my shoulders from sinking beneath his gaze. Confidence. I need to show confidence. "That's not why I'm here. It's more of a personal matter. Well, a bit of a legal matter too."

He furrows his brow; clearly, he wasn't expecting that. "What does that mean?"

"Do you have time to talk? It won't take long, but it's really important." I lower my voice. "The information is of a sensitive nature, so I'm not supposed to talk about it in front of others."

His jaw shifts back and forth, then his eyes flick to the clock on the wall. "Fine. After the lunch rush. I'll talk to you in the locker room. Wait there."

I try to hide my disappointment. That's at least two hours from now. But what else am I going to do? I nod, then go back to the locker room, taking a seat in one of the chairs. While I wait, I go over my story in my head. Confidence. That's all it takes.

My fingertips are sore from gnawing on them for two hours by the time I hear someone on the other side of the locker room door. I straighten as Mr. Evans enters and try to smile graciously. "Thank you for agreeing to talk. This means a lot to me. And to the investigation."

Mr. Evans pauses, frowning, before sitting on the bench in front of the row of lockers. "Investigation?"

I make my expression grave. "An upper Select who works at one of the other restaurants has gone missing."

"What other restaurant?"

I shake my head. "I'm not allowed to say. Not until the situation is made public. First, they need more information."

He eyes me, looking skeptical. "How is it you are involved in a legal investigation over a missing Select?"

"It's a long story, and I can't share the details. All I can say is that I know the identity of the last person who saw her alive."

"Alive? So this person is dead? Was she murdered?"

Good. He's alarmed. "I can't say, and I've probably already said too much. Since I know who saw her last alive, I'm considered a partial witness. I need to tell them everything I know about the suspect—I mean witness. I shouldn't call him a suspect. But he might have vital information about the victim's last whereabouts."

Mr. Evans' eyes widen. I hope I sound convincing. I can only thank my youthful fascination with precinct Reality shows if even a fraction of what I'm saying sounds right. "If this is a proper investigation," Mr. Evans says, "then why are you the one gathering information, rather than the investigators?"

I sigh. "Since I'm a probationary, I only get one chance to make my statement and I'm responsible for gathering all the information that supports it. If I'm missing anything vital, I could be penalized."

"Why come to me?"

"You're an important person in the restaurant community, I'm sure. You must know a lot of people at the other restaurants."

He shrugs, but I can tell his ego has been stroked.

"Do you know who supervises the cooks at the Golden Tempest?"

He squints, as if thinking, then nods. "Yeah. Aron Dwight."

"Who would his boss be?"

"The general manager is Chris Messinger."

I hide my grin. Names are good. "Do you happen to have contact information for either of them?"

He scratches the side of his head. "I think so. Are either of them a suspect?"

"I told you, I can't say. But I can promise you that getting their information may be instrumental in convincing the witness to talk."

He sighs, then reaches in his pocket for his reader. It's an older hologram model, nothing like my blocky reader, but not quite as fancy as something an Elite or upper Select would have. He taps the hologram, scrolling through blocks of illuminated text and icons until he stops at one. He gives me the contact code for the supervisor, then for the general manager.

I'm nearly bouncing with glee that my ruse has been successful and have to try with all my might to keep my face composed as I thank him for his time. I leave the locker room and exit the building, making my way to the Golden Tempest. Again, I lurk in the alleyway, ready to confront the first person who opens the back door of the restaurant.

This time, it's a young woman hauling empty boxes. I wait until she finishes stacking them against the wall before I make my presence known.

"Hi. Is Mitchell working today?"

Her eyes widen, her skin going a shade paler as she sees me. "You don't work here. What are you doing?"

I keep my tone nonchalant. "I'm waiting for Mitchell."

She narrows her eyes at me. "He's off today. He won't be back until Saturday."

I let my face fall. "Oh. I was hoping he was working today." I grasp my stomach, let my eyelids flutter. "I'm so hungry."

Understanding softens her face, followed by a heavy sigh. "He gives you food too? He's going to get us all in trouble if he keeps doing that."

"Does he do it a lot?"

"More than he should," she says under her breath. She eyes me a few seconds before taking a step closer. "Look, I really shouldn't get involved, but if you're hungry I can probably snag you a bread roll."

I shake my head. "No, please. I don't want to impose. Mitchell owes me, so I don't feel bad when he gives me left-overs. But I don't want to get you in trouble."

"Are you sure?"

"I'm sure. Mitchell will be here Saturday, though?"

"Yeah, he works the breakfast and lunch shift that day, I think."

Damn. I work until seven that day. "What about Sunday?"

"He's here all day Sunday. And it's our supervisor's day off." She winks at me, then returns through the door.

Three more days. I have to wait three more days to enact the rest of my plan, but I can do it. It's all I *can* do.

The alternative is wondering if Darren is still alive.

CHAPTER TWENTY-TWO

I return to numb so I can survive the next two days without losing my mind. On Sunday morning, I banish the numbness and find my determination instead. I get ready, then return to the city and the Golden Tempest. I find my spot in the alley. And I wait. I jolt upright each time the door opens, watching unfamiliar faces appear from behind it, taking out garbage, piling boxes. I won't approach anyone who isn't Mitchell or the girl from the other day. I don't want him to expect me.

The lunch rush comes and goes, and there's still no sign of him. I might have to request his presence after all. Another hour passes before the door opens again.

My breath catches in my throat when I recognize Mitchell. I approach him as he tosses a bag of garbage into the bin. "I need to talk to you."

He turns around, irritation flashing on his face. "You again? Tarla told me some girl was looking for me on my day off. What, are you stalking me or something?"

"Yeah. Now tell me about Darren."

He throws his hands in the air. "I already told you. I don't know—"

I take a step forward, turn the screen of my reader toward him. "Your supervisor, Mr. Dwight, that's his contact code, isn't it?" I pull my reader away, but not before he's able to glean a hint of what I've written in the text box. "He wouldn't like to learn about you stealing from the restaurant, would he?"

Mitchell presses his lips together, cheeks blazing. "I don't steal from the restaurant."

"You do," I say. "You give leftovers to Publics and probationaries. If that isn't stealing, I don't know what is."

He puts his hands on his hips. "Send the message. He doesn't know you. Without proof, it'll be nothing but a nuisance to him."

I pull my lips into an innocent smile. "I have proof. Darren told me about you and what you do for him. Your coworker also admitted to you giving food away."

"That isn't proof."

"It is when you're being followed 24/7 by invisible cameras."

His eyes go wide.

I take another step toward him. "You see, I'm a Reality candidate. I'm being monitored at all times, which means there is video footage of everything anyone has ever said in my presence. That includes Darren and your coworker. My lifestream may be inaccessible to any of us, but if a legal matter were involved, you can bet my footage will be under review. And if all that goes down, what will happen to you?"

"You're bluffing."

Another smile. "I'm not. I'm sure you're a nice guy, but I'm willing to do whatever it takes to figure out what has happened to Darren, even if that means taking you down with me."

Mitchell fixes me with a hateful gaze but says nothing.

I click the screen of my reader, pull up another contact. "I have Mr. Messinger's contact as well. Do I need to get the manager of the restaurant involved too?"

"What do you want?" he barks.

I lower my voice. "I want you to tell me what you know about Darren."

"I already told you—"

I raise my reader. "I already have the message drafted out. Do I hit send?" Slowly, inch by inch, I creep my fingertip to the screen of my reader.

"Stop!"

I pause just before it makes contact.

"I'll tell you."

Excitement ripples through me, followed by relief. "When did you last see him?"

"The last night I gave him food. Last..." He blinks a few times, as if trying to remember. "Wednesday. No, Thursday."

"You haven't seen him since?"

He shakes his head.

"Do you know his last name?"

"What, you don't?"

I feel heat rise to my cheeks, but I ignore it. "Answer the question."

"Yeah, it's Emerson."

Darren Emerson. I lock the name in my heart where it becomes a minuscule flame of hope. "He works two janitorial jobs in the city. Do you know where?"

He shrugs. "Veratech I think. Maybe Solaris-McMillan too."

Both tech companies. It checks out with what little I know. Two more facts about Darren. "Was he involved with anything that could have gotten him in trouble?"

"You mean besides you?"

I glare. "Me?"

"Yeah, you with your 24/7 monitoring." He says the words as if each one tastes like acid. "If he said such condemning facts about me, what did he say about himself? If he's in trouble, it's probably your fault."

I think back to the night when he was acting strange, recall the treasonous words spoken about the outlands and the faults of our government. What if someone *had* been watching? Someone important? What if he's being punished for what he said around me?

I feel nauseous, but I try not to show it. "Is there anything else you can remember? Was he acting strange at all?"

"No, can I go now? I have to get back to work."

I look from him to my reader. He gave me what I wanted. It may not be much, but it was something. I click my screen. Discard the message draft. My voice comes out softer. "Yeah. Thanks. I'm sorry for doing that, but I had to do something."

He turns toward the door and reaches for the handle.

"Wait."

He pauses, scowling. "What now?"

"Why didn't you just tell me right away? Why did you pretend you didn't know him?"

His eyes widen for a moment and his jaw shifts side to side. "I'm not supposed to say anything."

"What do you mean? Why? Who doesn't want you to say anything?"

"Let's just hope this little game of yours doesn't cost me my job...or worse."

I want to say more, but he swings open the door and pulls it shut behind him before I can. My head feels dizzy after such a heated conversation, and I prop myself up against the dumpster, closing my eyes as I replay the information I learned from Mitchell. What do I do with it next? Even with his last name, I doubt I'll be taken seriously if I try to report him missing. Do I go to Veratech and Solaris-McMillan and inquire there? Without clearance to enter the buildings, there's little chance anyone would speak to me. Do I see if Dr. Shelia can help?

My stomach churns at the thought, especially after how our last encounter ended. The things I said to her. But what other choice do I have?

I leave the alley and turn down the street that leads to the Select Health and Disease Prevention building when I remember Dr. Shelia isn't usually in the office on Sundays. I open my reader and pull up her contact instead.

Me: *I have new information about Darren.*

I keep walking, but my eyes constantly flick back to my reader until a new message comes in.

Dr. Shelia: *So do I.*

CHAPTER TWENTY-THREE

My heart feels like it's hammering my ribcage and will shatter my chest at any moment. Before I can compose my response, another comes in from Dr. Shelia: *I'm not in the office today, but I can meet you there in two hours.*

Two hours! That sounds like an eternity when I'm this wrapped in nerves. But I need to know what she's learned, no matter how long I have to wait. I wish she'd just message me what she knows. Does she finally believe me?

I have more than enough time to spare, but I can't help but rush to the Select Health and Disease Prevention building. Once inside, I take a seat in the brightly lit lobby on one of the plush chairs near the elevator.

My eyes are trained on the front door, and every person who enters the building makes my body grow rigid, hoping it's Dr. Shelia. The longer I wait, the more anxious I get. I can't keep the information I've learned inside me much longer. Part of me wants to rush immediately to the nearest precinct and report Darren missing. Or storm into his places of employment, regardless of my lack of clearance to enter the buildings. But both those plans are reckless and would likely get me nowhere.

Dr. Shelia is the one with the answers I need.

When I finally see her, I spring to my feet, forcing my legs not to break into a run. The building isn't nearly as busy as it is on a weekday, but I still want to maintain some measure of decorum. It doesn't help that I've been chewing my fingertips and bouncing my leg in the lobby for over two hours.

Her smile is grim when she greets me, and I try not to read too much into what that means.

"What have you—"

"Let's go up to my office," she says, then leads the way to the elevator. It's clear she doesn't want to share our news before then, so we ride in tense silence. We exit the elevator into the quiet corridor of the twentieth floor, then make our way to Dr. Shelia's frosted glass door. The clinic inside is dark.

She slides her keycard over the panel on the doorframe then enters. She slides it again on the inside and the lights come on.

I follow her behind the front desk and down the short hall to her office. When the lights turn on, I take my seat on the couch, legs trembling. I squeeze my hands into fists as I wait for her to put down her purse and jacket, then take her seat at her desk. Her eyes meet mine.

"I know his last name," I say. "It's Emerson. Darren Emerson. He works at Veratech and Solaris-McMillan."

Shelia watches me, her face blank.

I continue, my words coming out with an excited tremor. "He has a friend who works at the Golden Tempest. He's confirmed that he hasn't seen him since the night I last saw him, and someone didn't want him to talk to me. He'd purposefully withheld information about Darren from me. What did you discover? Do you know where he is? Do you know who took him? Why?"

"Claire." Her voice is firm despite how soft it is.

I hate the sympathetic look on her face. It can't mean anything good. "What happened?"

"I need you to take a deep breath and relax."

Relax? What does that word even mean in relation to this situation? How does she expect me to relax? I can't relax. I can't breathe deeply. I can't stop shaking. My frayed nerves are tearing apart every muscle, every bone. I need her to tell me what she knows before I explode.

"Maybe you should lie down."

"Just tell me."

She closes her eyes, as if she's the one trying to relax. "I watched your footage."

I can feel the blood drain from my face. That's not what I was expecting. "Wait...what? I thought you said you couldn't."

"I didn't want to get your hopes up. After what happened Wednesday, I contacted your agent and explained your situation. She got the footage for me and sent it."

"And? You saw him in the alley?"

She hesitates before answering. "No."

My heart sinks. "No? How is that possible? What did the cameras show? Did you at least get a look at his attackers?"

She shakes her head.

I feel like I'm going to faint. My eyes fall to the floor as I brace my hands on either side of my hips to keep from swaying side to side. When I lift my face, I meet Dr. Shelia's gaze. My voice comes out small. "Did you at least see when he left my apartment? Did he look...upset? Did he—"

"There was no footage of Darren in any of your recordings."

My stomach drops so low, I fear it will drag me to the floor. "That's impossible! What have the cameras been recording?"

"Just you."

A wave of anger washes over me as I imagine all the time I've spent with Darren while the cameras did nothing but record me. If this 24/7 monitoring is meant to provide entertainment, I can't imagine how that qualifies. "Is there audio with the footage? There could be some clue from the way he sounded in the alley or maybe the night he left my room."

"Claire, you aren't understanding. There was no footage of Darren, not because the cameras were focused *only* on you, but because there was no one else to be seen with you. Not anyone by Darren's description, at least."

I frown, tip my head back. "That doesn't make any sense. Maybe I didn't describe him to you right. He's tall, dark hair...wait, why should his physical description even matter? He's the one I've been spending time with. He's—"

"You haven't spent time with any man."

My eyes widen, my words stripped from my mouth. How can she be so daft? "Yes. I. Have."

Dr. Shelia leans forward and places her elbows on her knees as she plasters the most irritatingly apologetic expression I've ever seen on her face. "You aren't well, Claire. This man you've called Darren is nothing more than a creation of your imagination, like the night you saw your mother."

I rise to my feet. "This is nothing like when I thought I saw my mom. Darren was real. *Is* real, and he's seriously hurt. He's..." I pause, then take a step back, which only brings my legs against the edge of the couch. "Wait. You're in on it too. Oh my God, you're involved. You're keeping Darren away from me. Is it because of what he said to me that night? He was off his meds!"

Dr. Shelia sighs. "There is no conspiracy keeping Darren away from you because there is no Darren. I wish I didn't have to put it so bluntly, but this is becoming dangerous to your health. You're running around reckless after curfew, chasing a figment of your imagination, calling the attention of enforcers. I can't let you do this to yourself any longer."

Angry tears well in my eyes. "This is bullshit. This is such bullshit. I thought you were on my side."

"I am on your side. I can help you get through this. Lay down. Let's talk through everything."

I step to the side, inching away from her. "No. I'm never coming here again." I back toward the door, watching her as if she were an outlands viper poised for attack.

"Yes, you will. Otherwise, I'm going to have to intervene through whatever means necessary."

I turn and run, fling the door open, and round the corner into the hall toward the front desk. When I step into the waiting room, I freeze.

Dr. Grand rises to his feet, syringe in hand. His face is as blank as ever, eyes turned down at the corners. "I'm sorry, Claire."

I take a step away, then another. When did he even come in?

"You need to relax," Dr. Shelia's voice comes from behind me, followed by her hand landing softly on my shoulder.

I whirl around to shake her off, then feel a sting in the back of my neck.

CHAPTER TWENTY-FOUR

When I wake, I'm in an unfamiliar room. The walls are bright and white like Dr. Shelia's office, but there are no windows. Just the bare bed I'm lying on. I bolt upright, but the blood rushes to my head. I squeeze my eyes shut, waiting for the dizziness to clear. When I open them, the door opens too.

Dr. Grand enters.

I glower. "What have you done to me? Where am I?"

He closes the door behind him but doesn't come any closer. His metal case is in hand. "I'm not going to hurt you. I'm only here to run some tests on your vitals."

"You drugged me."

"I was ordered to sedate you. I'm sorry."

I laugh. "Sorry? I doubt that."

He studies me for a moment, the corner of his mouth twitching as if he wants to say something. His face remains blank, but there's that look in his eyes again, almost apologetic. But I can't believe there's any redeeming quality about this man. Not him. Not Dr. Shelia. "I'm going to approach you now and proceed with the checkup."

"Where am I?" I ask again, tensing as he moves toward me.

He approaches the bed and opens his case like he usually does at the end of my sessions with Dr. Shelia, removing the reader, the disks. "You're still at Dr. Shelia's clinic, but in the resting room."

"Where is she?" I flinch as he places a cold disk on one temple then the other.

"In her office. I'll have to tell her you're awake soon."

"What is she going to do with me?"

"Whatever she thinks she must do." There's a hint of bitterness in his voice. He places the remaining disks on me, then taps the reader to illuminate the hologram of my vitals. He lowers his voice, eyes on the image of my brain, the shifting column of numbers and letters on the side. "Don't fight her this time. If you go along with everything, it will be over a lot sooner."

"Over? What will be over? Is she going to kill me?"

Dr. Grand meets my eyes, his expression puzzled for once. "Kill you? No. It's not like that."

"What is it like, then?"

"I can't say. Take my advice though. Don't fight her. Do what she says." He sounds tired. Spent. I realize the circles under his eyes are darker than mine.

I shake the observation from my head. "Why should I listen to you? You aren't any better than Dr. Shelia. You're in on it together."

"You couldn't be more right or more wrong."

I sneer, irritation making my shoulder twitch. "What are you talking about?"

He turns off the hologram, then begins removing the disks. "All I can say is we're more alike than you think."

Another bark of laughter escapes my lips. "You? Like *me*? I hardly believe that. You're a doctor. That makes you at least a first rung Elite."

He nods. "I was. A fourth rung, in fact."

"Was?"

"I'm a probationary citizen now, like you."

I narrow my eyes. "That's the best you can do? A blatant lie?"

"It's not a lie. I'm a probationary, assigned to Dr. Shelia as my sentence."

I sneer. "Wow, I guess former Elites really are treated better than the rest of us, even after filing Forgiveness."

"It wasn't simply a matter of filing Forgiveness. I was convicted of a crime."

A chill runs down my spine. Why is he telling me this? I swallow hard. "A crime?"

He frowns as if he can tell what I'm thinking. "It isn't the kind of crime you're imagining. I didn't hurt anyone. I...five years ago, I worked in a private clinic here in the Select District. One of my patients was a little girl. She was dying. Elite medicine could have saved her. Time was running out, so I wrote her the prescription. I saved her life."

"How was that a crime?"

"Selects and Publics have to be on a waitlist for Elite medication and can't access it unless they receive special approval. I'm sure you know this."

I nod. My mom was on that waitlist for her lung cancer medication. She didn't have to wait long, though.

He continues. "Well, this little girl's family was first rung Select. Bottom of the list, ahead of Publics only. It was illegal for me to write the prescription without approval. Since I technically didn't steal it, I wasn't sentenced to prison. Instead, I was fined a hefty sum exceeding a lifetime's worth of income. You know what that means. Probation."

"Still, at least they sentenced you to something in your previous field. They went easy on you."

He shakes his head. "It isn't as easy as you think."

"Why?"

He looks away from me, his voice so low, I strain to hear. "There are things you don't know."

My eyes widen. Does he know something? About the truth? "Like what?"

He ignores me and continues packing the briefcase, then snaps it shut. He turns toward the door.

"Wait." I scoot off the edge of the bed, find my footing on unsteady legs, then take a step forward. "Do you believe me? About Darren?"

He pauses, fingers around the door handle. "I believe things have been very hard for you and are going to get harder. Do what Dr. Shelia says. Things can get far worse than you can even imagine."

Was that a threat? Or a warning?

Without another word, he opens the door and shuts it behind him. I follow but find the handle locked. My eyes dart around the room, seeking any form of escape. Not a minute passes before footsteps sound outside the door, followed by the turning of the handle. I back away as Dr. Shelia enters.

"I'm not going to hurt you, Claire. Have a seat on the bed."

Dr. Grand's voice echoes in my head. *Do what Dr. Shelia says. Things can get far worse.* I don't take my eyes off her as I return to the bed and take a seat.

"How do you feel?"

"How do I...feel? How do you think I feel?"

She looks at the reader in her hand. "Your vitals seem stabilized, although I can't say they look good. But your pulse seems normal. Cortisol only slightly elevated. I'd say you feel better than you did earlier today."

I glare. "I'm trapped in a windowless room against my will after being sedated. And you think I feel *better*?" At least earlier, before I came to see Dr. Shelia, I had hope. Now I'm only angry and confused.

"Well, your anxiety is gone, is it not? Check in with your body, your lungs, your chest. You can breathe easier now. Your heart isn't racing."

She's right. I may be furious but the feeling that every inch of me is raw nerve waiting to explode has dissipated. My mind is clear. "Did you do something to me?"

"I had Dr. Grand administer your antidepressant medication while you were sedated."

I bite my lip to keep from lashing out. Heat rises to my cheeks.

She takes a few steps closer to me. "I want you to come see me first thing every day so Dr. Grand can administer your medication. Before work and on your days off. No exceptions. I also want to add an extra session together each week."

I shake my head. "No thanks."

She pinches the bridge of her nose. It's the most flustered I've ever seen her. When she meets my eyes there's a hard look in them. "I didn't make myself clear. I'm not asking you. I'm telling you."

"And I'm telling you no. I'm not taking that medication and I'm not coming to see you every day." I stand. "Can I leave now? Or are you going to sedate me again?"

"Claire, you don't have a choice in this." Her voice is shaking, as if she's fighting to reel back either tears or rage. "This has gone far beyond where I can ethically allow things to go without intervening. You are a danger to yourself and to others. I know this is hard for you to hear, and right now you don't trust me. I understand. Honestly, I do. But if you don't let me help you, I have to turn you over to the peacekeepers."

My eyes go wide. Peacekeepers. The enforcers in white. She's saying I'll be...what? Taken to a sanatorium? Tears glaze my eyes. "Do you actually think I'm crazy?"

"You have experienced significant trauma." Her voice is even again. Soft. "It isn't uncommon for someone with your history to develop psychosis. Please let me help you. I don't want to lose you. Both as a patient and as someone I care about."

I want to argue, to roar, to scream. She doesn't care about me! She couldn't possibly! This is still all part of the grand plan to keep me and Darren apart. Or is it? The sympathy in her eyes looks so real. But how can I trust it?

I'm again reminded of what Dr. Grand said to me earlier. Whatever the case, he was right. Things can get far worse for me.

My words come out with a tremor. "Can I at least see the video footage first?"

Dr. Shelia's face falls. "I wish you could, but you can't. I'd do anything I thought would bring you closer to healing. But I can't allow you to break the terms of your probationary sentence. I could lose my job."

My eyes fall to the ground. I force my bottom lip to quiver. "Couldn't you at least ask? Ms. Wan gave you permission to watch it. What if she could get the same permission for me?"

She sighs. "I could request special permission."

I lift my eyes to meet hers. "Thank you! You still have the footage, right? You didn't delete it? Please save it. Please. In case your request is approved. I need to see it as soon as possible."

She presses her lips into a firm line. "I don't want you getting your hopes up. There's almost a zero percent chance you'll be allowed to watch it."

"But you *do* still have it?"

She nods. "I've saved it with your files on my computer. It isn't going anywhere. I do wish you'd trust me, though."

I turn my head away from her, fighting to shift my grin into a pained expression. "Maybe I can start to. I don't know. I'm so confused about all of this."

"But you will agree to come here daily for your medication? And I want to add a second appointment each week in addition to Wednesday. How about every Sunday, on your day off?"

I give a reluctant nod.

"Good. I'll send our new schedule to your reader." She watches me for a few seconds, then approaches and lays a hand on my shoulder. "You're going to get through this. I promise."

I meet her eyes, trying not to scowl. "Thanks."

"You can head home now. Your backpack is in the waiting room. Do you feel all right to walk to the rail alone?"

"Yeah, I feel good." It's true. Despite my annoyance that I'm being forcibly medicated, I can't help but appreciate how calm and clear it's making me feel.

"I'll see you tomorrow morning, then."

I leave her clinic and check my reader on the way down the elevator. I've been there for four hours at this point, most of it sleeping off the sedative. When I exit the building, I see a mes-

sage pop up on my reader. It's the new schedule from Dr. Shelia. I'll be coming an hour before work every workday morning,
and at 9 a.m. on my days off. Even on Sundays, when my meeting with Dr. Shelia doesn't begin until an hour later.

Ideas are forming in my head, hazy and without a well-de-
fined path, but at least my end goal is clear.

Somehow, I have to get into Dr. Shelia's computer.

I might know someone who can help me.

CHAPTER TWENTY-FIVE

Instead of going straight to the rail, I head to the Salish.

Molly won't be off work for at least another two hours, so I wait by the back door. I've been doing that a lot lately. I suppress a laugh.

As I wait, I look over my new schedule again and again, committing it to memory.

My eyes are heavy by the time Molly enters the alley. I straighten when I see her, and she stops short. Her eyes go wide. "Claire?"

I put my hands in my pockets and close the distance between us. "Hey."

"How have you been? Is your hand okay?" Her words come out fast and eager. It pains me, realizing how worried she must have been. I never thought to contact her before now. Some friend I am.

Then again, I've had other things on my mind.

"Yeah. My stitches are already starting to dissolve."

"Are you still working?"

"Just at the hotel. Can we walk to the rail together?"

"Sure."

We start walking. Out of the corner of my eye, I can see Molly watching me. "Is everything okay? Like, *really* okay?"

I shake my head. "Remember that guy I told you about? Darren? Something happened to him." I tell her everything I can without getting too far into the details. I tell her about my meeting with Mr. Evans, my well-constructed lie, followed by my confrontation with Mitchell. I tell her about Dr. Shelia, the footage, and Dr. Grand's warning.

Molly seems most concerned about my conversation with Mr. Evans. "Let me get this straight. You basically hinted that Mitchell was a potential suspect in a missing person's case?"

I shrug. "It isn't far from the truth. I just stretched the details. And I never told him the name of the person in question, just where he worked and that he's a cook."

Molly looks at me with a combination of admiration and horror. Her expression turns to concern. "Damn, I hope you didn't get Mitchell in trouble. Word can travel fast if Mr. Evans thinks he has a good piece of gossip to spread."

"Do you know Mitchell?"

"A little."

I face her, take her by the shoulders. "Do you know Darren too?"

She pulls her head back, eyes wide at my outburst. "No, Claire, I don't"

I let go of her, shake my head. "Sorry. I'm a little jumpy. I feel like I'm losing my mind."

"Isn't that what your psychiatrist thinks?" She offers me a sympathetic smile, the kind that looks more like a grimace. "Do you think there's a possibility that it's true?"

"No. There's no way I imagined Darren. Dr. Shelia is part of something and I'm going to prove it. I need to see that footage. There's something on there she doesn't want me to see."

"How do you know? What if she's right? What if she really didn't see Darren in your footage?"

I appreciate that she didn't say, *what if you really are crazy?* I know that's what she's thinking. Can I blame her, though? Just hearing my words out loud makes me question my sanity. "I'll know if I see the video."

"How are you going to see it if she won't allow you to?"

We've reached the rail platform. I look around, finding it almost empty aside from a few tired citizens. Not a single enforcer in sight. I lean toward her and lower my voice to a whisper. "That's where you come in. You still know how to code?"

Her eyes narrow with suspicion. "Yeah. Why?"

"Is there something you can do to override touch recognition on a computer?"

"You want me to break into your psychiatrist's computer? That's not coding. That's hacking."

"Can you do it?"

Her mouth falls open, and she's looking at me like I really have lost my mind. "Do you have any idea what kind of trouble that could get me into? I'm already on probation."

My stomach sinks. I hadn't thought of her safety at all when I came up with this plan. What's wrong with me?

She steps closer, eyes wide and glazed with tears. I've never seen her so frightened. "We could both get in trouble for even talking about his. The cameras, Claire! Are you trying to get me killed?"

Her words remind me of what I said to Darren the night he was acting crazy. Is that what I seem like to her now? I put my head in my hands and cry into my palms. My voice comes out muffled. "I'm sorry. I'm so sorry. I don't know what I was thinking."

I feel her hand rub my shoulder. "It's okay. Let's put it behind us. You weren't thinking straight. You didn't mean it." She says it loud, as if her words are meant for someone else. Maybe they are.

I shudder, again wondering if the things Darren said when in my presence were the reason he was taken. Am I next?

Molly and I sit in silence on the rail, then walk to the housing centers together, like Darren and I did so many times. I wish we would have included Molly in those walks. Then I'd have someone to prove Darren is real.

When we part ways, I go to my room and fall into a deep sleep almost as soon as my head hits my pillow.

In the morning I wake and return to Dr. Shelia's office, right on schedule. She greets me with a curt nod, then calls in Dr. Grand.

I accept my shot of medication.

Go to work.

Go to sleep.

Repeat.

Numb. Hopeless. But I don't stop plotting. Planning. Forming ideas in my mind that still can't seem to get me from where I am to where I want to be. For now, all I can do is watch. Wait. Ask.

On Wednesday I go to Dr. Shelia's clinic twice. Once before work and once again for our regular meeting. In the morning, Dr. Shelia isn't there. Just Dr. Grand. He leads me to the windowless room instead of the office.

"Where is Dr. Shelia?" I ask as I roll up the sleeve of my shirt, exposing my shoulder.

"Her office hours don't begin until 9 a.m." Dr. Grand takes the syringe, places an ampoule in the chamber, locks it in place.

I watch as he presses his finger a few times to the chamber's screen.

"What does that do?"

He looks up as if surprised by my curiosity. After a moment of hesitation, he turns the syringe until the tiny screen faces me. The panel is fully lit green. "Dosage," he says. "You receive a full dose. If, for example, we need to increase your dosage, we'll need an additional ampoule but not all of it. This allows me to control how much is delivered per ampoule. A partial dose would show a fraction of the screen lit green to correlate with the dose given."

I nod, and he takes that as permission to proceed. I feel the sting in my shoulder. Intramuscular injection, Dr. Grand called it the first time. After two days of these daily injections, I'm still not used to the pain. "Is Dr. Shelia tired of watching over your shoulder? Is that why she isn't here today?"

"She's only been here the past two mornings to make sure you arrive. I suppose you've earned her trust already."

Good.

I go to work, fall into a mindless laundry routine. Ignore the chatter. Scrub stains. Load sheets and blankets into the enormous machines. Fold everything in neat, perfect rows.

Numb.

Plotting.

Watching.

I return to Dr. Shelia's clinic after work and sit in the waiting room until it's my turn. Emily takes me back to Dr. Shelia's office. Once I'm closed inside, alone, I stare at the desk, eyes locking on the metal circle where the touch sensor that activates her computer is located. The door opens and I jump.

"How are you feeling?" Dr. Shelia asks as she enters the room and takes a seat in her chair.

"Fine."

"Sleeping?"

I nod.

Before she can say anything else, I slide off my shoes and lay back on the couch.

"Claire—"

I take a deep breath. "On August seventeenth I was walking home from the rail. I was scared, because it was so late. Tired, because I hadn't been sleeping. I heard footsteps behind me, which scared me even more. It was so dark, my eyes were playing tricks on me. I saw something on the street corner, then heard my mother's voice. She was a hallucination, but I was entranced by it. I almost got hit by a bus. Someone saved me. That's when I met Darren Emerson."

Dr. Shelia isn't pleased, but she doesn't stop me, either. I spend our entire appointment recounting everything I remember about Darren. When the hour is up, I sit, put my shoes back on, and thank her for her time.

In the morning I return. Fall back into the same routine.

Meds.

Work.

Sleep.

Meds.

Work.

Sleep.

Every chance I get, I study Dr. Shelia's desk, trying not to seem too anxious whenever I catch her activating her computer. A press of her thumb. The keyboard and screen holograms illuminate. Does the screen only respond to her touch too?

I'm still at a loss for ideas, but I don't stop watching. Learning. Plotting.

Saturday, it's just Dr. Grand.

Meds.

Work.

Sleep.

On Sunday morning, I accept my injection in the resting room, then sit with Dr. Grand in the waiting room until Dr. Shelia arrives for our new meeting. There's no time alone in her office like there is on Wednesdays when Emily walks me back to wait for her.

We begin our session. I pick up where I left off, launching into every detail of my first kiss with Darren.

Sleep.

Meds.

Work.

Repeat.

Repeat.

Wednesday again. This time, after Emily walks me into Dr. Shelia's office and closes me inside, I pause by Dr. Shelia's desk. I don't have long before she will be in to begin our session, so I quickly press my thumb over the sensor. Nothing. Not even a warning beep. I press it again. It isn't anything I didn't expect.

I am on the couch before the door handle begins to turn.

It's more of the same today. This time I'm pouring every detail of my first night with Darren, our passion, our lovemaking. Dr. Shelia pinches the bridge of her nose, not in distaste, but in frustration. Still, she doesn't stop me.

These meetings with her are the only times I feel any sense of control. They are the only experiences in my routine, medicated, numb life that remind me I'm not crazy. That I once was happy. That I felt love and it was real.

I'm *not* crazy.

But even being sane is wearing on me. There's still no solution. I still have no idea how to get into Dr. Shelia's computer. All my memories of Darren aren't bringing him back from whatever dark place he's being kept. If he's even still alive. How long has it been since I last saw him? I hate how sometimes when I think of him, certain memories are becoming blurred at the edges. Those memories are like a cloud in the sky shaped like something so uncannily familiar, until it begins to shift and transform into nothing more than a white blur. Like it never was what you first saw it to be.

I replay those memories most often. I won't lose them.

I'm lost in one of these memories, head pressed against the window of the railcar as it lurches into motion from the Public District platform. It's all I can do to keep from obsessing over the fact that Darren has been missing for over three weeks. I watch the sun rise over the buildings as the Select District comes into view. It's Sunday. Back to the clinic. Back to another meeting with Dr. Shelia. I've cycled through my memories numerous times already. I think today I'll start from the beginning again.

The weight shifts next to me, shattering my thoughts. The empty seat has been filled, but I don't look.

"Hi, Claire."

I jolt upright, turn my head, and lock eyes with Molly. I'm taken aback at first. I never see her on the rail in the morning.

Her lips are pulled into a sad frown. "How are you doing?"
I can't even force a smile. "Fine, I guess."

"Hang in there, okay?" She presses her palm into mine, entwining our fingers. It's the most intimate gesture she's ever given me, and it makes my eyes water. "I'm here for you."

"Thanks," I croak. We stay like that all the way to the city. As soon as the rail comes to a stop, she springs from the seat without so much as a goodbye. I'm frowning after her, frozen with confusion, when I realize I need to get up too. I stand, my palm still warm from Molly's hand. But there's something other than warmth left in it.

My eyes catch something round and silver before I close my fingers over it and hurry off the rail.

I don't know what the little disk will do, but I can guess.

CHAPTER TWENTY-SIX

I feel a rush of excitement as I walk toward the Select Health and Disease Prevention building, my mind spinning to form a plan. Dr. Grand should be the only one there when I arrive at eight, and Dr. Shelia won't be in until nine. Last Sunday, Dr. Grand administered my injection, then gave me the option to wait in the resting room or the waiting room until Dr. Shelia arrived. I chose the waiting room. Even though, like the resting room, it has no windows, its expanded space and furnishings make it seem less like it's closing in on me.

That gives me an idea.

I enter the lobby of the building, then ride the elevator to the twentieth floor. Inside the clinic, Dr. Grand sits behind the front desk. He greets me with a nod, then leads me to the resting room.

I take a seat on the bed as Dr. Grand prepares my injection site. My eyelids flutter as the cool antiseptic touches my skin, and I grasp my stomach with my free hand.

"Are you all right?"

I squeeze my eyelids shut and nod.

"Do you need to lie down before your shot?"

I offer a shaky smile. "No, I'm fine. Just nerves, I think. I guess I'm still not used to needles."

"If you're sure." I don't redact my statement, so he proceeds with the shot. When he's finished, he disposes of the needle and empty ampoule, sets the empty syringe aside, and faces me. "Would you like to wait in here or the waiting room?"

"Waiting room, please." I stand from my seat on the bed but falter as my feet touch the ground. I right myself before I topple to the floor, then stand, swaying as I bring my hand to my forehead.

Dr. Grand comes to me, eyes wide with concern. I've never seen such a departure from his normally vacant expression. "What's wrong?"

"I don't know." My words are choppy, strained, as I stumble to the waiting room. "I'm lightheaded. Water."

He runs to the water dispenser next to the desk where he fills a paper cup, then hands it to me. I drink it back in a single gulp, so he fills another. "You should sit," he says.

I look at the chairs, then around the room. My chest heaves, my breathing growing shallow. "I need air," I gasp, fanning my face. "A window."

"There are no windows." Dr. Grand waves his hand, indicating the walls around us.

"Dr. Shelia's office." I sway again, then gasp for air. "She has a window. She opens it for me when I get like this."

He doesn't respond at once. My heart is racing. He knows. He knows I'm lying. Finally, I hear a sigh. "I suppose I can let you in there."

I inhale a wheezing breath. "Please."

He leads me to the closed door leading to Dr. Shelia's office. I continue to sway, eyes closed, listening to Dr. Grand sliding his badge against the keypad, hearing the opening of the door. I stumble into the room and make my way to the far wall, where I lean next to the window. As Dr. Grand opens it an inch. I lurch forward, letting the air fill my lungs.

"Do you feel better?" he asks after a few minutes.

"A little. Can I just lay in here until Dr. Shelia gets in?" It's a long shot. I know he's going to refuse. Of course he'll refuse.

He doesn't answer immediately. "Fine."

I press my lips into a tight line to hide my surprise as I shuffle to the couch and sink into it, tossing my arm over my eyes.

"I should take your vitals."

"No," I groan. "I just want to be left alone. Please."

He hovers before me, and I am certain he's going to insist. This isn't going to work. There's no way it will work. He sighs. "Very well."

I don't open my eyes until I hear his footsteps enter the hallway. Several minutes pass before I sit and hazard a glance at the door. He left it open, but I don't see him waiting in the hall. I watch for another few minutes before I spring toward the desk. With trembling fingers, I reach into my jeans pocket and retrieve the disk. I set it next to the touch sensor. It's almost exact in shape and size. With a deep breath, I place the disk over the sensor. Nothing happens.

I press my thumb over the disk.

The keyboard hologram illuminates, followed by the screen projection, which is nothing more than a blank, blueish glow. My mouth falls open. I glance at the door again, then place my finger at the center of the screen, like I've seen Dr. Shelia do many times before. The lack of sensation when I touch the hologram surprises me. It's been years since I've used a hologram device myself. I'm so used to glass beneath my fingers these days.

The screen responds, goes from pale blue to a pale yellow with numerous bright icons. My heart is racing as my eyes try to devour as much information as I can. What am I looking for? She said she kept the video with my files, so there must be something with my name on it in here. I look everywhere but see no search option.

I glance at the door again. Sweat is beading at my brow, pooling beneath my armpits as I read and reread the names of the icons again and again. Think. Think! When I was an Elite, how did we navigate these types of computers? I close my eyes, think back to the one year of Elite schooling I had. I try to place myself in my memories. How would I have searched?

I open my eyes, place two fingers in the middle of the hologram and flick them outward. The screen blurs and a search bar opens. I seek out the correct keys on the keyboard, spell my name. Enter.

A file icon pops up. I click it open. More file icons. I read the titles beneath them. *Background. Probationary sentence. Contact. Parents.* I swallow the lump in my throat and read the next. *Appointment notes. Medications.* The last file is unlabeled.

Another glance at the door.

I click the icon.

The screen is swallowed by an image of my face, multiplied from six different angles. Then one of the angles shifts to the vaguely familiar face of my probation officer, Marcus Smith, and another shifts to Kori Wan. There's no sound, which I'm grateful for. I can't attract any attention to what I'm doing. At least not until I find the proof I'm looking for. My eyes dart from one image to the other, then watch as the images again fill with different angles of my face. A shiver crawls down my spine. There's something unnatural about seeing myself on video. Like it isn't me at all.

The footage follows me as I leave the office and enter the dark streets. I know what will happen next. I'll stop at the corner, check my reader. Find my apartment for the first time. Try to sleep. Wake up the next morning and explore my neighborhood before coming here for my first appointment with Dr. Shelia. I don't need to see any of that. I need to see the night I met Darren.

I touch the screen, seeking the control icons. The date and time of the recording pops up on the bottom left. I touch the screen again, and a second hologram pops up and forward, partially overlapping the screen. I see the speed symbol and click it until the images move at maximum pace. I watch my first few days of my new life fly by, only slowing the speed to double when I recognize the date at the bottom left. August 17th.

I watch me walking down the dark streets, shoulders hunched, eyes seeking left and right. Darren was right when he did his impression of me that night. I look like a maniac.

I slow the speed again, returning it to normal pace, when I see myself pause. This is it! This is where I think I see my mom. I'm not surprised there is no sign of her, just an empty corner littered with garbage bags. I see myself cross the street, see the lights of the bus rounding the corner. My heart races. Here it is. Darren will jump in at any moment...

I watch as I freeze in the middle of the street. Then I leap away, crashing into the sidewalk where I lay still.

I can't blink. All I can do is stare. Where is Darren?

Where the *hell* is Darren?

I see myself huddled on the ground, then watch as I rise, dust myself off. Half the images show a different angle of my face, eyes vacant as I stare. I'm mumbling something, but I can't hear what I'm saying. The other images show my surroundings. I'm alone.

I glance at the door. With hands that shake like never before, I touch the control hologram, seek out the volume. I increase it just enough to hear what sounds like crazed muttering.

I shake my head. Rewind. Watch again. Listen.

Again, all I see is me. I hear the bus this time, and my squeal of fear as I leap away, hear myself whimpering as I huddle on the sidewalk.

I watch it again. Again.

Then I click the speed icon and watch what remains. Days and days go by. Days filled with me mumbling and muttering to myself. Sometimes I seem to be speaking out loud. Other times I'm sitting on my bed, staring at the opposite wall, eyes empty.

Sometimes I open my apartment door, but no one is there. I close it. Open it again. Close it. Sit back on my bed.

I watch myself work, ignore Molly, chat with Molly, stare at the wall while I'm at the sink. Watch as I steal a bag of leftover food from the kitchen after work. Watch as I fold laundry, chat with the other women, stare at what I folded. I watch myself on the bus, my eyes fluttering closed, head landing on the shoulder of the stranger next to me. He shrugs until I move my head, and I stare out the window instead.

I watch myself on the rooftop, face toward the sky for hours at a time. Watch myself in bed, staring at the ceiling. Watch as I confront Mitchell. Watch as I run down an empty alley, then as I lead the enforcer to the abandoned laundromat.

The footage ends shortly after, and I watch it again. I increase the speed, then slow it back down, increase again, hoping something will change what I see.

It's the same. More of the same. Same, same, same.

Crazy.

Insane.

This woman is not me. This can't be me.

I don't hear when Dr. Shelia comes in, don't realize I'm sobbing, don't hear that I'm screaming. I don't feel my knees hit the floor or Dr. Shelia's arms wrap around me. I'm shaking. Or she's shaking. Or rocking. She's rocking me.

And I'm falling apart, piece by piece.

CHAPTER TWENTY-SEVEN

I don't know how much time has passed before I realize I'm lying on the couch in Dr. Shelia's office, blotting tears from my face. Even without uttering a word, I can tell my throat is raw from sobbing. My mind is starting to clear, and with it comes renewed pain, horror.

Shame.

I close my eyes against the tears, but they don't come. I've spent them all.

"Take all the time you need," Dr. Shelia whispers.

I turn my head toward her, then my eyes fall to her desk. The disk Molly gave me is no longer there covering the touch sensor.

Dr. Shelia opens her hand, reveals the piece of metal in her palm. "Are you looking for this?"

I avert my gaze to the ceiling, heart beating high in my chest. She'll report me now, I know it. I knew she would when she found out what I'd done, but I thought I'd have proof to throw back at her. Not this. Not this terrifying realization.

She closes her fingers over the disk. "I'm not going to ask where you got it."

"When will they come for me?" My voice is high-pitched, nothing like what I'm used to sounding like. I hate how much it sounds like the girl from the video footage.

"When will *who* come for you?"

"The enforcers. Or peacekeepers."

She leans forward. "I'm not turning you over to anyone. Not the enforcers, not the peacekeepers. I'm here to help you.

I always have been. You've broken a major restriction in your probationary sentence by viewing your footage, not to mention hacking into my computer. But you aren't well. You can't be blamed for the measures you've taken."

"Because I'm crazy."

"I think it's much more nuanced than that. You've gone through a major trauma, and as a result, you haven't been sleeping. You've developed depression. This resulted in a neurochemical imbalance that has led to psychosis."

"Sounds like the definition of crazy."

"Let's not focus on that part," she says. "Let's focus on why your psychosis developed the way it did. Are you ready for that?"

I shrug.

"We know what happened with your mom. We know the effect her death had on your mental health. Let's explore this idea of Darren."

I shudder, feel a twitch in my shoulder that makes me want to lash out with fury.

"Breathe, Claire."

I'm shaking again, so I take a deep breath, then another. Another.

When I'm breathing easy, she continues. "You created this image of safety, of love. This image led you to deeper happiness, peace, and trust."

But it wasn't real. I can't bring myself to say this out loud, though. The rage floods through me again, but I quell it faster this time.

"You see, Claire. You saved yourself from that bus. That was *you*. Yet, as we've already discussed, you hadn't learned how to love yourself. You hadn't accepted that your mother's sacrifice was worth anything. That your life was worth anything. So your subconscious mind created a circumstance it was more willing to believe, and your conscious mind accepted it. It was easier to believe someone else saved you. But even then, the truth came out. The *someone* you created fell in love with you, and you loved him back. Do you know what that means? You loved yourself all along."

Her words hardly make sense, so I don't try to process them. Just listen.

She continues. "He only disappeared when your conscious mind was ready to accept the truth. That you are worthy of love. You didn't need that buffer anymore. But your subconscious still rebelled. It wants to stay sick to protect you from something. It *fears* being healthy. Why do you fear being healthy?"

I shake my head. "I don't know what you're talking about. I don't know what any of this means."

"That's okay. We'll take it slow. Forget all about Darren, for now. Start small. What's the first thing that would happen if you got healthy?"

I deepen my breathing to keep the rage at bay. "I would...I don't know. I would sleep."

"And if you slept?"

"I'd feel better throughout the day, I guess."

"And if you felt better?"

"I'd work better. Maybe I'd work more."

"If you worked more?"

I frown. Where is she getting at? "I'd pay off my debts faster. I'd get off probation according to my original plan."

"And then what?"

"I'd move up in the rungs. Work more. Eventually be a Select again."

"Then what?"

"Then...I don't know. I'll get married, have kids, and die."

"Do you want that?"

I open my mouth, but my words feel stuck in my throat.

"Let me put it another way. Why don't you want to become a Select again?"

The words aren't stuck after all. They are fighting to come out, but I won't let them. Can't let them.

"You can tell me, Claire."

"Because I hate it! All of it. The whole system." The silence that follows my outburst is deafening.

"Tell me more."

"I don't want to be a Select. I don't want to be part of this game, this city, anything. It's flawed, it's broken, and I hate it. I'll never beat it. I'll never be an Elite. I'll never be anything of worth to this system, and I hate that. My parents finally became something, and they were killed for it. Sure, it was an accident. But how does this system treat victims of such accidents, even victims of their esteemed Elite? By punishing them. It's disgusting." I'm gasping for breath, then go silent again, stunned by my tirade. These don't sound like my words. They sound like Darren's.

Then again, according to Dr. Shelia, Darren *was* me.

I fight the rage.

"It's safe to feel that way. You aren't the only one."

I face her again. It takes all my willpower not to scowl. What would she know? She's an Elite! But my rage isn't meant for her. Not anymore. Not when she's the only one who can help me.

"I was once a probationary, Claire," she says. "Long, long ago. I was just a couple years older than you. I know what it's like to feel like you are drowning beneath your probationary sentence and to feel like the system is against you. But I played the game, as you called it. I fought to move higher. Higher. Became a Select. Worked in tech. Made the right connections. Worked seven days a week to put myself through medical school. I've only been an Elite for ten years, but it happened for me. I was willing to do what it took to get here. That doesn't mean I pushed myself to collapse like you've done. It means I played to my strengths and protected my weaknesses. The long game."

"Why are you telling me this?"

"Because I know how you feel. I know that rage. I know what it feels like to want to give up, to let the darkness of your situation take you. You don't want to try because you don't see the point. Being a Select isn't what you want, it's what you think your mother wanted. And you don't think you'll ever be an Elite. But I want you to think bigger. As big as you can. That is how you'll get out of this."

Her words stir a flicker of hope inside, but it's nothing more than a spark compared to the vast emptiness I feel.

Dr. Shelia flutters her hand dismissively. "I'm sorry if I've gotten carried away with this conversation. You can hardly see straight right now, I'm sure. I just care about you so much."

Her eyes are glistening. How did I ever think she was against me? I swallow the lump in my throat.

"We will work on this," she says with a smile. "I promise. You'll be on the other side in no time." She rises from her chair and I move to do the same, but she gives my shoulder a gentle press. "Rest as long as you like. I can even have Dr. Grand sedate you, if you'd like."

A sense of warm relief washes over me at the thought of slipping out of consciousness. I never thought I'd actually desire the prick of a syringe. "Yes."

CHAPTER TWENTY-EIGHT

When I return to the world of the living, I find Dr. Grand in Dr. Shelia's chair. He helps me to sit, then checks my vitals like he does at the end of all my appointments with Dr. Shelia. The dim light coming in through the window tells me the sun is setting. "Is Dr. Shelia still here?"

"No," he says. "She's returned home. She wanted me to tell you she is going to be here every morning for your daily injection and has reserved her first hour of every day to speak with you."

I feel a familiar rage ignite in my chest, but I breathe it away. Dr. Shelia isn't the enemy anymore. She never was. "That's probably for the best."

"She also said you can message her anytime." I'm struck by the flat tone of his voice, the slightest hint of a bitter edge. Perhaps it's because she went home and left me in his care for the better part of a perfectly good Sunday. It was probably supposed to be his day off.

After he's finished recording my vitals, he walks me to the lobby of the building. "Are you well enough to get home on your own?"

I nod. It isn't like there's anyone to contact. Molly, maybe. But I can't face her. I can't tell her that all her hard work to help me only made me realize I'm crazy. Then again...shouldn't I be grateful for that? That I now know the truth?

I try not to think about anything on my way home. Not the footage, not my memories of Darren, not the consequences of my psychosis. Nothing.

When I sleep, I dream of the video footage playing before me, expanding on a massive screen as tall as my apartment building. Behind me, another enormous video begins to play, this one showing events the way I remember them. I stand between the two, suffocating as they press closer around me, squeezing the air from my lungs as they flatten me between them. I try to make it out, but they've merged at the edges, creating a cage. With a scream, I'm pulled into one video, then another. One leads me deeper, head underwater. The other leads out a door to fresh air. I know this, yet I can't decide which one does which. I can only struggle.

I wake to the alarm on my reader, gasping as if I'm coughing up water. Memories surge, and I can't fight them this time. Darren's words. His face. It's so clear. So clear. How could he have been part of my imagination?

I all but run out the door, my mind brimming with questions, teeming with evidence that I can't correctly place. I'm biting my nails all the way to the city, down the streets, and in the elevator to Dr. Shelia's clinic. Once inside, I see Dr. Shelia and Dr. Grand waiting for me, and I have the sudden urge to run away. My mind won't clear, but I know I must get away from them. I turn toward the door.

"Dr. Grand!" Dr. Shelia's voice is a command. I'm in the hall, halfway toward the elevator, when I feel a prick in the back of one calf, then the other. I fall to my knees, legs numb, thrashing my arms as Dr. Grand sweeps me up and brings me to Dr. Shelia's office. An injection in my forearms stops me from flailing, and he sets me on the couch. I alternate weeping and screaming as Dr. Grand places another injection in my shoulder.

A few minutes later my head is clear. I look from Dr. Shelia to Dr. Grand. "What's going on?"

Dr. Shelia offers me an apologetic smile. "We are going to have to increase the dosage of your medication. It wore off much sooner than usual."

I try to sit but can do no more than shift side to side. "Why can't I move my arms or legs?"

"We had to sedate you," Dr. Shelia says.

"Then how am I awake?" I look at Dr. Grand, but he says nothing.

"The sedative is usually administered in the back of the neck," Dr. Shelia explains. "But when injected in quarter doses at the extremes of each limb, it keeps your body immobile. Your medication has helped clear your mind by stabilizing and balancing the neurotransmitters in your brain."

"How long am I going to be like this?"

Dr. Grand finally speaks. "It will wear off in less than an hour. You should be able to go to work after this just fine."

"Are you comfortable starting our session?" Dr. Shelia asks.

I nod. Dr. Grand steps back but doesn't leave. Instead, he stands against the wall behind me. In his hands, there's a tray holding four syringes. More sedatives?

Dr. Shelia sees where my attention has gone. "It's a precaution, nothing to worry about. Now that we've increased your dosage, we need to keep an eye on its effects. If it wears off again, we'll need to sedate you and get you on an antipsychotic instead of an antidepressant."

Antipsychotic. I shudder.

"Can you tell me what prompted you to get so upset this morning?"

I squint, trying to remember the teeming thoughts that boiled over when I woke. Some rise to the surface. "There are things that don't add up. Even after seeing proof, part of me can't let my suspicions go."

"Don't be so hard on yourself," Dr. Shelia says. "It's going to be a long time before you will be able to fully believe he wasn't real. In the meantime, treat it like a game. Get curious. Explore. Ask. Now that we've upped your dosage, you shouldn't spiral out of reality like you did this morning.

Spiral out of reality. Looking back, that's certainly what it felt like. I try to detach from my memories, instead examining them like they're an interesting book. "The first thing that came to mind this morning was Mitchell. I never knew anything about him until Darren told me his name, where he worked. How is that possible?"

Dr. Shelia doesn't look surprised. "Mitchell works in a restaurant, as did you. It's possible someone mentioned him in passing at work, and your subconscious picked up on it, filed it away to support your fabrication. Does that sound plausible?"

I feel the tightness in my chest loosen. Didn't Molly say she knew Mitchell? What if she talked about him to me before when I wasn't paying attention? "Yeah, I guess so." Another question comes to mind. "But Mitchell said he knew Darren. He said he was told not to tell me anything."

"You did threaten him, Claire. Did he admit to anything you didn't personally prompt him to?"

"His last name, his places of employment." I blush when I realize I all but gave him that information. I told him he worked janitorial at two places in the city. He only gave me names of two tech companies. Places I don't have access to.

And he knew I didn't know Darren's last name. He could have said anything, and I'd have believed it. "Oh," I whisper.

"Whoever you heard about Mitchell from, probably mentioned him giving food away. You were right about that when you confronted him. You played on a very real fear of his. Don't you think he would have said anything to get you to leave him alone, including play up some sense of danger about speaking to him?"

I nod. It all makes so much sense. How did I not see it before? The terror of my morning fades, and I return to a calm numb. We continue our conversation until the sedative wears off and I'm able to move again. Dr. Grand takes my vitals, then helps me to my feet. I test my footing. Steady.

"You're doing well, Claire," Dr. Shelia says, rising to her feet. "It may not feel like it right now, but you are already making incredible progress. You can allow your Darren memories to remain without guilt for now, but I do want you to start digging for your true memories, if that feels comfortable."

"Okay." It feels daunting. How do I find my true memories when my ones of Darren are so persistent?

"It will take time," Dr. Shelia says as if she can read my mind. Then she does the unexpected. She embraces me. "Be patient with yourself."

Her touch brings tears to my eyes.

"I'll see you tomorrow," she says when she pulls away.

I wipe my eyes and smile. "Tomorrow."

I leave the building and head to work. Outside, the world seems different. Clearer. I feel trampled, beaten down at the bottom of a dead-end alley. At least I can see my way out. It's far. But I can see it.

CHAPTER TWENTY-NINE
Now

"Is your mind wandering, Claire?"

Dr. Shelia's voice brings me back from thoughts of Darren to the brightness of her office. "Sorry."

"Are you ready? We don't have to do this now if you aren't. You can keep your Darren memories as long as you need them."

I take a deep breath. "No. I'm ready." This time, I think I mean it. I can't count the number of appointments I've come to with this same goal in mind, only to leave trembling and gasping for air.

"All right, then. Think about him from the beginning. Tell me what you remember."

I tell her. I watch the memories in my mind's eye and explain them in every detail I can muster. His crooked smile. His warm hands. His kiss. His caress. I no longer feel pain when I recall these things. I feel nothing. It's like I'm watching footage of a stranger's mundane life. There's nothing interesting to see here. It just is what it is.

When I finish, Dr. Shelia asks, "Are these memories of Darren real or false?"

I don't hesitate, don't cry out. I only feel a slight twinge in the back of my shoulder. "False," I say with confidence.

"Now let's go back once again. Tell me what your real memories are."

I return to the dark street on the way home that fateful night. I remember my terror, my racing pulse, how muddled my thoughts felt when I hallucinated seeing my mom. This is where my true memories deviate from the false ones. I remember seeing the lights of the bus and leaping out of the way. I can almost feel that flash of panic as I dove for the sidewalk, taste the tang of blood in my mouth from where I bit my lip upon impact. When I stood, my mind became muddled again. This is where I created Darren in my false memories. But in reality, I stood trembling, mumbling.

I continue replaying my memories from there, explaining everything to Dr. Shelia in minute detail. Some things are still fuzzy around the edges, but not nearly as fuzzy as my Darren memories, which are more like an old, tattered cloth at best. For the most part, I remember what it was like to live in a constant state of shock, putting on my best brave face for the world, while inside I was struggling to reconcile the truth of my situation.

I remember Molly telling me about Mitchell when we waited for the rail together. It was the night I was imagining meeting up with Darren, so I was too distracted to pay much attention to what she was saying, but I remember the conversation now.

I remember sitting for hours at a time, weaving beautiful fantasies of love and passion. I remember eating my stolen meals—meals I'd taken from my own place of work—alone on the rooftop. That's where I'd talk to myself, laugh to myself, as if I were my best friend in the world. I was.

I remember trying to let Darren—who I knew was false—go. It was the night I imagined us sleeping together. That night on the rooftop, I stared at the sky while living a glorious fantasy in my head. It was meant to be a goodbye. I thought I was ready, but I wasn't. Letting him go shattered my hold on reality even more, and part of me clung harder and harder. I remember what I did after. What it was like to weave a conspiracy between me and everyone who tried to help me see the truth. I didn't want to see the truth.

I remember watching my footage, feeling like my entire being had been hewn in two. I remember Dr. Shelia spending the last few months putting me back together. Now I'm whole. Healthy. Turns out, numb *is* healthy after all.

When I finish, I smile and turn my head toward Dr. Shelia.

"Which memories feel more real to you?" she asks. "The Darren memories or the other ones?"

"My real memories are far clearer. The Darren memories are almost laughable." It's true. How could any of that have happened? How could some random stranger leap in front of a bus at the perfect moment? How could he have fallen in love with me so quickly? How could I have done the same with him? I made my life into a fairy tale so I didn't have to come to terms with my reality.

Dr. Shelia clasps her hands and brings them to her heart. She's beaming at me like I'm the cleverest girl in the world, and she's my proud mother. In a way, she's become like a mom to me. She'll never replace my real mom, of course, but I feel like she's healed a part of me I never thought would mend. She swivels toward her desk and presses the touch sensor, then taps a button on her keyboard. She calls in Dr. Grand.

For the first week after Dr. Shelia upped the dosage of my medication, Dr. Grand would wait behind me with a tray of sedatives, just in case. He never needed to use them. The new dosage worked. Whenever I needed to work through some line of thought that triggered suspicion, I would talk to Dr. Shelia about it instead of freaking out. You'd think by now he'd be as proud of me as Dr. Shelia is, but as he walks into the office, he wears nothing but that blank expression. Same as always.

He opens his case, goes through the routine motions of placing the familiar disks on my face and scalp, then picks up his reader. The hologram of my brain and vitals illuminates behind me, but I don't bother looking. I've never learned to decipher anything about it, even after all these months of daily visits. It seems to take longer than usual for him to come to his conclusions as he types furiously on his reader.

"She's done it," he finally says. I can't help but hear the disappointment in his tone.

I meet his eyes, cock my head. "What did I do?"

Dr. Shelia stands, looks over his shoulder at the reader. "She has. She's replaced her memories."

I shake my head. Shouldn't she say *recovered*, not replaced?

Dr. Shelia locks eyes with Dr. Grand, gives him a subtle nod. He clenches his jaw before setting the reader in the case and removing the disks from me.

There's a tension in the room I can't ignore. "What's going on?"

Dr. Shelia's smile is so wide, it's almost terrifying. I've never seen anything this close to excitement coming from her. She rushes to her chair as Dr. Grand sweeps from the room. She taps her computer screen hologram, moves two fingers from the center, and brings up the search. She types something too fast for me to see, then the screen shows what looks like a video.

My breath catches. Is it more footage? Was I caught doing something I shouldn't? My mind races to make sense of what it could be, but I'm more confused when the video begins to play. It isn't my lifestream footage. It seems more like footage from a curated show.

The title fills the screen, *Twisting Minds*, followed by a rapid succession of images that look like the one I just saw of my brain. I barely register when Dr. Grand returns and stands at my side. I can't tear my eyes from the video.

A voiceover says, "Can a healthy mind be twisted?"

Then it's Dr. Shelia's smiling face on the screen. "Hello. I'm Doctor Geraldine Shelia, top psychiatrist and Reality star. And I'm here to prove that the answer is yes."

My stomach churns as I look from the screen to Dr. Shelia, then back again. The voiceover returns. "A controversial new Reality program is coming to you. These probationary Reality candidates—"

Several images of faces flash by, including my own. Another face sparks recognition. The man I'd seen leaving her office in distress all those months ago?

"—are unknowing participants in this twisted series that exposes the strengths and weaknesses of the human mind. Tune in daily to watch the progress of Twisting Minds." The title returns, then fades away.

Dr. Shelia presses the sensor on her desk, and the screen and keyboard disappear.

I stare dumbly at the empty space where the screen was, trying to collect my bearings. Before I can stop it, my body begins trembling from head to toe. I squeeze my fingers into fists to find some sense of control. "What was that?"

"You've made it, Claire." Dr. Shelia is still smiling. "We've finally completed your story arc. You were a tough one. The last to hold out, in fact. I was starting to worry nothing would convince you Darren wasn't real. But everyone has their weakness. Yours was physical proof."

My chest is heaving, throat tightening. Tears spring to my eyes. "I don't understand. What have you done to me?"

"What you mean is, what have we done *together*? The answer? Something great. We've come to a conclusion about my hypothesis. Can convincing someone they are crazy actually make them crazy? The answer? Yes." She sounds nothing like the woman I've gotten to know over the last several months. She speaks faster, louder. Her eyes are wide and glittering with excitement.

There's only one thing I need to know. "Was Darren real?"

Dr. Shelia's mouth falls open. "That's still your main concern? Even after all this time?"

"Answer me," I say through my teeth.

"Well, yes, but you never would have met him if it weren't for me and my team working together with Santoro Corp. They're the corporate sponsors for his probationary sentence, the ones providing experimental drug testing."

"He wasn't testing antidepressants?"

"Yes, and then some. Together, we tested an antidepressant that releases certain hormones under remote command. We constructed your schedules, your proximity of living arrangements. We planted the hologram of your mom, the timing of the bus rounding the corner, the trigger of adrenaline when Darren saw what was about to happen to you. When he saw you the first time, we triggered a rush of dopamine, serotonin, and oxytocin, and continued to trigger that same hormone cocktail every time you were together."

He knew. I remember the night he was acting strange, how he didn't want to take his pills because he felt like they were doing something to him. He was right, and I didn't believe him. I swallow hard. "Did you do the same to me? With my medication?"

"No." She laughs as if it's funny. "You were dosed with real antidepressants and sedatives. I needed your vitals as close to normal as possible to prove my hypothesis. Besides, we knew you wouldn't need help falling in love with him. Not with your history."

It dawns on me, and I feel like I might pass out. "You really were responsible for him going missing. Why? Why did you take him? What did he do wrong?"

She looks at me like I'm daft. "He didn't do anything wrong. It was the next step in the experiment. I needed you to stop trusting yourself, to question your sanity. To have the truth of your reality contrast with logic. His time in the experiment ended when you saw him in the alley."

I'm choking on the question, but I need to know the answer. "Is he...dead?"

"My goodness, Claire! It's like you think we're monsters!"

"Where is he?"

"He's safe. That's all you need to know."

Safe. But what does that mean? How does that word fit into this situation at all? "I was never crazy," I whisper under my breath.

"Well, you are now."

"What do you mean?"

She points behind me, and I turn to find the hologram of my brain has remained illuminated. "Once you accepted the

Darren lie, your brain began to experience negative neuroplasticity, resulting in significant reduction of gray matter, white matter abnormalities, overactive dopamine and cortisol, and severe changes in the hippocampus. Through believing the lie that you suffered from psychosis and consequently changing your memories to serve that belief, you became exactly what I was convincing you that you were."

I shake my head, feeling like it will explode as I try to put her words together. "But I'm not crazy. I know what was real!"

"Do you, Claire?"

I blink, two sets of memories barreling down on me. My head is spinning, my blood boiling with rage. "What about the footage I saw? That's the *only* reason I started to believe this lie!"

"I let you believe the video was real, not the product of your footage heavily edited with a body double. The special effects crew did an excellent job with that, I must say. I knew you'd never believe the video was real unless you found it on your own. Telling you that you couldn't watch it ended up being the best way to convince you to gain access to my computer. I knew you'd find a way to hack it eventually, although I never guessed you'd have a friend help you."

I remember Dr. Grand's presence and look up at his looming form. I see what he's holding. It's his tray of sedatives; four syringes lined up in a neat row. One for each limb. "You knew too. You let me into her office the day I hacked her computer. You knew what I was going to do. That's why you let me stay in there alone." Looking back, it was all too easy. "You lied about everything. You aren't a probationary."

Dr. Shelia throws him a hard stare. "You told her about your status?"

He flinches slightly. Maybe he didn't lie about that after all. "It didn't break any rules of production. I wanted her to know."

It's too much. I can't handle the weight of everything I've learned. I feel like I did when I watched my footage, on the brink of complete emotional and mental collapse. "What have you done to me? What have you done to Darren? You've destroyed us! Broken us!" I'm screaming. Wailing.

"It's all in the name of science," Dr. Shelia says. "Dr. Grand. Now."

He barely moves before I spring away from him and his tray of sedatives.

"No!" I shout. I'm surprised when he pauses. I look from him to the tray. "Please, no. I'll calm down, I promise. Just give me a moment. Then I'll do whatever you want."

He looks to Dr. Shelia. I watch her out of the corner of my eye. She gives a subtle nod. Dr. Grand takes a step back and I return to my seat. My breathing is labored, eyes squeezed shut as I fight to take in everything I've heard. What does this mean for me? What can I do?

It becomes clear.

My breathing grows heavier until I'm gasping for breath. I sway, then open my eyes, seek out Dr. Grand. "Water," I gasp. "I need water."

He nods, looks to Dr. Shelia.

"Get her some," she says with irritation.

Dr. Grand sets his tray on the corner of Dr. Shelia's desk, then hurries out of the room.

I'm still gasping as I face Dr. Shelia. "Air. Please, I can't breathe."

She narrows her eyes at me, then gives them a roll. "Fine." As she swivels her chair to face the window, my eyes lock on the sedatives. She rises, takes a step.

I grab a syringe.

CHAPTER THIRTY

I lunge for Dr. Shelia's legs, stabbing the needle into her calf with all the force I can manage. The screen is partially illuminated with green. A quarter dose. I press the sensor at the end of the chamber

She shouts and collapses on the leg. As she bends to remove the needle, I stick another one in her opposite shin. Press the sensor. I retrieve the syringe as she struggles to remove the first, then leap out of reach of her swinging arms. Her movements are sloppy, exaggerated, making me think the sedative has reached higher than just her legs. She's finally able to remove the first syringe and tosses it away from us. I don't bother to go after it. Instead, I press the screen of the partially used one until the bottom turns green, ready for another quarter dose.

I grab the remaining two from the tray on her desk.

"Where's Darren?" I demand as I advance toward her. "Tell me now or I'll stick the rest of these in you at once."

Her eyes are wide as she struggles to drag herself away from me toward the wall. "That would kill me."

I offer her a smile, wave one of the syringes. "Exactly. Tell me where he is."

"Dr. Grand!" Her eyes lock behind me.

I shift to the side, so my back is to neither of them. Dr. Grand is in the doorway, paper cup in hand, watching us with his blank expression. My stomach sinks, but I don't move. I knew this was unlikely to work, but that doesn't mean I'll go down without a fight. I'm sizing him up, considering the best place to stick him with a needle...

"Dr. Grand!" she shouts again, her tone pitched with rage. "Why are you standing there? Sedate her!"

His eyes fall to the syringes in my hand, then move to Dr. Shelia. His expression shifts into something I don't understand. Is it amusement? "I can't," he whispers.

"What do you mean, you can't?"

"It goes against the Ellis Law. I'm both cast and crew. My contract specifically forbids me from interfering with any of the Reality candidates in a way that counteracts the goal of the experiment."

Dr. Shelia tries to wave an arm my way, but all it does is rise a few inches before flopping to the ground. "You think *this* isn't counteracting the experiment?"

He shakes his head, then looks me up and down as if he's appraising a painting. "No. This is exactly what you wanted to see. This is the sum of your experiment, of the Twisting Minds program. What will the subjects do as a result of the experiment? How will they react? How badly will they break?"

"Dr. Grand, you are misinterpreting your contract," she says through clenched teeth. "I'm the one who had it drawn up. Now sedate her!"

He takes a step back. "I can't. The law forbids it."

"So, you're just going to watch as she abuses me?"

"I've been watching you abuse her and many others over the last several months." His tone is flat, empty. "This isn't any different. It's all science, isn't it?"

Desperation flashes over her face. "Dr. Grand, please."

He takes another step back, then another. "Don't worry. I'll call for enforcement." Then he's gone.

I'm so shocked, I can do nothing but stare at the empty doorway until movement catches my eye. I round on Dr. Shelia, watch her give up on her feeble attempt to reach the syringes in my hand. She falls back, then returns to her previous goal of scooting away from me. I spring forward and ram the partially used syringe into her shoulder. I press the sensor, and the arm goes limp. The other struggles to reach across her torso but can't. I stick the next needle in her upper thigh. I press the screen until it turns entirely green. A full dose, but I don't press the sensor.

Only one syringe remains in my hand. Another full dose.

"I'm not kidding, Claire." Dr. Shelia's words are coming out slow. "If you release any more sedative into my body, you will kill me. I don't have the tolerance you do."

I kneel beside her. "And I'm not kidding either. I don't care if it kills you. If you want to live, tell me where Darren is."

She laughs. "Why do you care? He never loved you. Your relationship was fabricated by me and my team."

My shoulder twitches and I feel a surge of rage. I clench my empty hand into a fist. "It doesn't matter. You said it yourself, I didn't need any help falling in love with him. What I felt was real."

She smirks. "What exactly are you going to do if I tell you where to find Darren? Break him out?"

I furrow my brow. Break him out...does that mean he's imprisoned? I wrap my fingers around the syringe in her thigh, my thumb hovering above the sensor. "Answer me."

She rolls her eyes. "He's at the Rainier Public Sanatorium. Happy now? If you'd like I can give them a call, I'm sure they'd be more than pleased to reunite you before the enforcers lock you in a cell for the rest of your life." Her voice is laced with venom.

My heart feels like it's splitting in two. "Why is he at the sanatorium? You said his time in the experiment ended after I saw him in the alley. That was months ago!"

"He may not have been my subject in the same way you were, but the experience shattered his reality almost as badly as it did yours." She says this without a hint of guilt. In fact, I'd say there's pride flickering in her eyes.

It's taking everything in me not to press the sensor.

Dr. Shelia lowers her voice, an odd smile stretching her lips. "I'm sure this is about to be the most popular episode of Twisting Minds yet when it airs. And I can't imagine the sheer volume tuning in to your lifestream right now. Think about that. Think about everyone watching."

It's a threat. I should back off. I know it. I've already gone too far. She told me where Darren is. He may be broken, but at least he's safe.

There's that word again. *Safe.* There's no such thing as safe anymore.

"I'll make you a deal," she whispers. "Take these out and I'll defend you against the enforcers when they arrive. I have that power. Nothing is unforgivable in the name of entertainment and science. That's how I got you out of jail the first time, remember?"

I can't speak. All I can do is watch my thumb as it trembles above the syringe, begging my fingers to move away, then silently screaming at them to press the sensor.

She continues. "We have amazing chemistry. You have no idea. We are magnetic on the screen together, unlike any of my other subjects. I can see you have a knack for the dramatic. You could be a star like me, not just a subject. The audience already loves you. Let's end this on a powerful note. You move away and start sobbing. We'll talk through your pain until the sedative wears off. That's when I'll wrap you in my arms. Cut scene. The audience will love it."

I glare. "I'm not doing this for attention."

She nods. "I believe you. Trust me, I do. But that's the magic of it. You have the chance to move from unwilling participant to star. In no time, the popularity of Twisting Minds will pay off your probationary sentence. You'll bypass Public, Select. You'll go straight to Elite, and you'll get to act side by side with me. I'll make a part for you in season two."

My eyes go wide. "There's going to be a season two?"

"Of course there is! You may have been the final subject to crack, but the experiment is far from over. There are still unlimited other ways to prove my hypothesis. I have so many other ideas for people of different ages, backgrounds. There's a little girl, age six, I'm in negotiations over. I can't even imagine how pliable her young mind is." Her voice crawls higher with excitement.

I feel nothing but cold. Empty. She's going to do this again. And again. And again. "How could you consider doing this in the first place, much less a second time? Do you have no conscience? No care about what you're doing to us? What you've done to Darren? What you've done to me?" My voice has risen so loud, I'm shouting now. "What you're going to do to a six-year-old girl?"

Her mouth falls open. "You and everyone else should be proud you were allowed to be involved with something so important."

"We should be proud?" Rage courses up and down my body, burning me. "Proud? Proud to be treated this way?"

"You're treated better than you should be. You're a probationary. You have no rights."

A fire is burning in my chest, propelling my words. "I should have rights. We *all* should have rights. You're no better than me, just because of your status."

She laughs "You can tell yourself that all you want, but that's not the reality. I've been there. I've been a bottom-feeding probationary. And I became *this*. I have no pity for the worthless like you."

I shake my head. "You're wrong. I'm not worthless. I'm worth so much more than this." My mom's words echo in my head. *Rise up, my sweet one. You are worth more than this.* Maybe I've always misunderstood what she meant by them when she came into my room, whispered in my ear, kissed me as I fell back to sleep. Maybe not. But I know what they mean to me now. "I'm worth more than this. We *all* are worth more than this. You can put whatever label you want on us, but you will never change that. We will rise in ways you can never imagine."

"Oh, get over yourself," Dr. Shelia says. "You think you're a revolutionary? A rebel? No. You are property of the United Cities of America, and you are nothing."

A tear rolls down my cheek. I tighten my grasp on the syringe in her thigh. "You're wrong. And I can't let you hurt more people."

Her eyes go wide with realization, the color draining from her cheeks. "You can't possibly...you'd be a murderer!"

I lean in close, bring my lips next to her ear. My voice trembles, but I can't tell if it's from rage or sorrow, as I whisper, "I plead insanity."

I press the sensor.

The final syringe finds her neck.

CHAPTER THIRTY-ONE

I close my eyes and let the subtle motion of the truck sway me. Even with my hands bound behind me, I'm surprised how quickly I get comfortable. The seat cushion is plush, the backrest firm but shaped to contour my spine. I can almost pretend I'm not in the back of a peacekeeper truck headed to a sanatorium.

"Breaking news, Seattle!" a cheerful female voice rings out. I don't need to open my eyes to know it's coming from the screen hologram at the back end of the truck. That's something I've nearly forgotten about the Elite city. There are screens everywhere. The bathrooms. Street corners. The rails. The busses. Jail cells. Sanatorium transport trucks.

The voice continues. "Our favorite little murderer has been released from the Bellevue Elite Prison and is on her way to Bellevue Elite Sanatorium." The reporter then adds in a light-hearted undertone, "Which we all know is basically luxury rehab."

"That's you!" says the peacekeeper next to me. I open my eyes and see him pointing a white-gloved hand at the screen.

I shudder as the screen flashes a photo of my mugshot, followed by a video showing the crowd of reporters who swarmed me less than an hour ago outside the prison as I was led to this truck. The contrast is stark between the me from an hour ago—well-rested, dressed in the white, loose clothing of someone belonging to a sanatorium, hair brushed and pinned neatly back—and the me from my mugshot. There my eyes are red from crying and the dawning realization I'd murdered someone, my skin pale and haggard, my hair in blond streamers around my head.

The memory of the night the enforcers found me huddled next to Dr. Shelia's body, rocking back and forth, sends a ripple of nausea through me.

The news host, a pretty brunette with wide, blue eyes and swollen, red lips, continues. "Citizens have been in an uproar ever since Dr. Shelia's murder and Claire Harper's subsequent verdict of being found innocent on the grounds of insanity. Some citizens think the Twisting Minds project went too far. Others think Claire did."

A man's fat, flushed face appears on the screen. I only met him once, but I recognize him as the prosecuting attorney from my trial. "Claire Harper had no rights. She should have been put to death immediately, not given a trial."

The news host makes a comical buzzing sound in the back of her throat. "Wrong answer!"

The image shifts to the familiar face of the defending attorney, Ms. Martha. We had several meetings, but most of her work was done outside my presence since I wasn't allowed to attend the trial until the end. I sit upright, curious. "At the time of the crime, Claire Harper's lifestream had soared in viewership, earning her enough credits to pay off her probationary sentence. Even though she didn't know it at the time, she was a Public citizen, giving her the right to a fair trial. And all the evidence is clear. Claire Harper acted during a psychotic episode, brought on by the trauma of the Twisting Minds program. She cannot be held responsible for her actions."

Another familiar face shows on the screen. "Claire Harper had undergone severe prolonged emotional and mental stress,"

Dr. Grand says. "She was prone to outbursts of rage, impaired judgment and mental faculties, and the inability to distinguish fantasy from reality. It is well documented in her lifestream, the Twisting Minds program, and in my professional notations."

The news host returns. "Dr. Grand underwent a short trial regarding his refusal to help Dr. Shelia when Claire attacked her, but he was found innocent under the Ellis Law and the terms of his contract as cast and crew of Twisting Minds. The popularity of the show has paid off his probation and allowed the reinstatement of his medical license." She smirks and raises a well-penciled eyebrow, then frames the side of her mouth with one hand as she pretends to whisper, "I'm sure it didn't hurt that he was team Claire, if you know what I mean."

The screen shows a white vehicle moving down a busy freeway, and I realize it's the truck I'm in. "And for all you hopeless romantics, you better believe our little Claire has already put her newly found wealth and fame to good use. That's right folks. As we speak, she's on her way to Bellevue Elite Sanatorium, where dear Darren has already been transferred from Rainier Public. Her first act upon being declared innocent was to pay off her estranged lover's probationary financial sentence. Even though their wealth has raised them to Elite status, both require continued mental care."

The image returns to the news host who has her hand to her heart, which is essentially a deep valley of cleavage above her red top. "Are you swooning, Seattle? Stay tuned! We'll update you on the reunion in less than an hour."

My heart races. Less than an hour. I'm going to see Darren in less than an hour. If my arms were free, I'd bite my nails.

One of the peacekeepers sitting across from me leans forward. I can't see his eyes through the black lenses in his white helmet, but his posture is casual. "Can I have your autograph later?"

. . . .

AS THE TRUCK COMES to a stop, my breaths become shallow. The back door opens, and a swarm of sound and movement attacks my senses. Reporters are shouting my name, and I see flashes of movement belonging to cameras that rove around my head, their familiar whir and buzz making my stomach clench. I have to remind myself these aren't the same cameras that used to hound my every move. Those ones are gone. Gone.

"Get back," the peacekeepers demand. There are six in total who were in the truck with me, and there are six more marching toward us. Together they make a sort of moving tunnel for me to duck through as we make our way into the building. Once the doors close behind us, the cacophony cuts off and is replaced with soft instrumental music. We're in a bright, white hall, unornamented aside from the occasional cutout in the wall where a small green plant sits. The peacekeepers continue to flank me, but they spread out as we make our way to the front desk at the far end of the corridor.

"Claire Harper," a female voice says at my side. I jump, locking eyes with the woman from the news program. "I'm Mara Laine. I appreciate you giving us this exclusive into your reunion with Darren. How do you feel?"

I open my mouth, but I'm too overwhelmed to talk. Instead, I train my eyes on the desk ahead, where a small retinue awaits. Several men and women in white uniforms—nurses, I guess—stand before the desk with gentle smiles. Sticking out like a sore thumb is my agent, Kori Wan, in a neon green jumpsuit to match the green streak in her black hair. She squeals as I approach, tapping her black spiked heels with excitement.

"Claire! I'm so happy to see you! You look much better than last time."

Last time. She must mean when she came to remove my tracker and cameras. This makes me grin, remembering the look of nausea on her face from having to meet me in a Public jail cell. I'm sure, in retrospect, she wishes she'd waited a week to remove the tracker. That's all the time it took for my lifestream earnings to shoot me directly from Public to Elite citizenship and provide me with a private room at the Elite prison. Now those earnings can get me a new agent, instead of the one who sold me to Dr. Shelia. I force myself not to bare my teeth at her, and instead I make a mental note to fire her soon.

The peacekeeper beside me steps forward and presses the sensor on the cuff at my wrists until it beeps and falls away.

"Come," Kori says. "Let's get you all checked in. You're going to love it here. Ugh, I'm so jealous."

It's a strange thing to say about a sanatorium, so I raise a brow.

She makes a face like I'm daft. "You're going to meet so many celebrities."

I roll my eyes, then accept the holographic reader one of the nurses hands me. Scrolling to the bottom, I sign my name with my fingertip.

Kori takes it from me and gives it back to the nurse. "Done. Now for the fun part. Is your team ready, Mara?"

Mara Laine gives an exaggerated thumbs up, and a few cameras—larger than the ones I used to have—begin to circle me.

"I hope you don't mind that I gave Mara Laine the exclusive," Kori says. "This is going to be huge. Your lifestream has already reached the top of the replay charts, and your final episode of Twisting Minds bumped out Hunter Ellis' suicide as most watched episode! Can you believe it?"

I blanch.

Kori rounds the desk to the short hallway beyond, beckoning me to follow. "The people love you. Darren too! This is going to be hot."

Darren. His name makes my heart leap into my throat. I want to feel excited. Happy. But I don't. I'm terrified.

Kori leads me, Mara, and two of the peacekeepers to a closed door at the end of the hall. I hold my breath as she opens it.

More bright walls greet us on the other side, but the lighting is warm and dim. Not dim like the lighting in the Public District, but like the glow of a candle. The sound of water grabs my attention, and I see a small pond beneath a layer of glass on the floor to my left. Tiny fish dart around inside it. Men and women in white, loose clothing like mine lounge in chairs around it, chatting animatedly. Behind them, a woman paints next to a hologram of a fireplace. I can feel its warmth from here. I take in the rest of the room, seeing an array of people engaged in various activities. But none of them are Darren.

I feel a hand on my arm and leap to pull away when I realize it's Kori. "He's waiting over here."

She leads us to a less populated section of the room where a long, white couch faces a window overlooking a green bamboo garden. I gasp. I haven't seen that much green in years. Then my eyes find the figure sitting on the couch, and I freeze. The couch is facing away from us, so all I see is the back of his head. But I know it's him.

I begin to shake from head to toe, sweat beading behind my neck. Ever since I made the decision to pay off his probationary sentence and have him transferred here, I've been in a constant state of fear. Will he be happy when he sees me? Angry? Indifferent? How will he see me? As someone he used to love? As someone he was forced to *think* he loved?

Or as a murderer?

Then another thought comes to mind. What if he turns around, and he's nothing like I remember him? What if his face is wrong? His smile skewed? What if this is just another trick and the man on that couch is a stranger? My head is spinning, and my knees are going weak. I take a step back, preparing to run. I can't do this. I'm not ready.

Then he turns his head to the side, and I feel the breath catch in my throat. I can't move. I barely hear Kori calling Darren's name.

He stands and turns to face us. Our eyes lock.

I'm shocked by the hollowness in his cheeks, the lines beneath his eyes. He looks worn. Broken. *What did they do to you?*

As he walks toward me, his expression shifts, but I can't read it. I don't want to read it. What if it says anger? Irritation? Or worse. What if it says apathy? What if Dr. Shelia was right? What if he never truly loved me?

Then a corner of his mouth lifts and everything becomes clear. My racing thoughts go still. My heart leaves my throat and returns to my chest. My legs regain their strength. I can feel my mouth mirroring his.

The way he says my name is like a caress. It sounds exactly how I remember it. His lips break into a full smile—the kind no twisted experiment could ever erase from my memory—and just like that, my world is back. And he's standing in front of me.

About the Author

Tessonja Odette is a young mother living in Seattle. Young, meaning 30-something. It's the new 20, right? Tessonja has always loved to write. Her wild imagination and fascination with the great unknown led her writing into the realm of fantasy. She writes books that inspire and expand the imaginations of others. When she isn't writing, she's watching dog videos, having dance parties with her daughter, or pursuing her many creative hobbies.

Read more at tessonjaodette.com.

Made in the USA
Monee, IL
01 February 2020